WITHDRAWN

BORR⬤WED
TIME

GREG LEITICH SMITH

with illustrations by LEIGH WALLS

Clarion Books >< Houghton Mifflin Harcourt >< Boston   New York

Clarion Books

3 Park Avenue, New York, New York 10016

Copyright © 2015 by Greg H. Leitich

Illustrations copyright © 2015 by Leigh Walls

Clarion Books is an imprint of Houghton Mifflin Harcourt Publishing Company.

www.hmhco.com

The text was set in Mundo Sans.

Library of Congress Cataloging-in-Publication Data

Smith, Greg Leitich.

Borrowed time / Greg Leitich Smith.

pages cm

Summary: "In this time-travel adventure, Max Pierson-Takahashi and his friend Petra
return to the days of the dinosaurs, where they must survive attacks from deadly prehistoric creatures and a vengeful,
pistol-toting girl from the 1920s"—Provided by publisher.

ISBN 978-0-544-23711-7 (hardback)

[1. Time travel—Fiction. 2. Dinosaurs—Fiction. 3. Survival—Fiction. 4. Science fiction.] I. Title.

PZ7.S6488Bo 2015

[Fic]—dc23

2015013600

Manufactured in the United States of America

DOC 10 9 8 7 6 5 4 3 2 1

4500561191

For Cynthia, my Muse. Always.

CHAPTER

I

NATE

LABOR DAY WEEKEND, 1985

"IT'S A *RACE*," NATE TOLD HIS BROTHER. "THE POINT IS TO *RACE!*"

The pair had just finished their heat in double sculls in the Labor Day Regatta on the Colorado River in Bastrop, Texas. Their boat, the *Velociraptor,* rested upside down on stands in front of the boathouse. The pair was hurriedly wiping it down to clear it out of the way of the high school crews.

The race itself had gone well, and the brothers had made it through to finals tomorrow. They didn't make it as the lead boat, though, and as far as Nate was concerned, that was because Brady had slacked off at about the three-quarter mark.

"The point is to win," Brady answered, gesturing with his rag. "The heats don't matter."

Nate made a choking sound and resisted the urge to strangle his brother. Not for the first time. The two were fraternal twins, and people said they saw the family resemblance only after they were told this. In contrast to everyone else in the family except their mother, Brady was blond and gray eyed. He was also the only one of the family who didn't need corrective eyewear. And he was good at almost everything, which only sometimes bothered Nate. Strangely enough, most people who met Brady liked him.

But to Nate, the bigger issue was that this was going to be their last regatta together. Brady had announced last night that he was giving up rowing to join the football team. "The hours are better," he'd said. "And so are the girls."

Nate tossed his rag into its bucket. "And what's wrong with winning the heats?"

"Nate," his brother said, with not quite a sigh, "I knew we were going to make it, so why burn ourselves out ahead of finals tomorrow, when it actually matters?"

Nate didn't answer as they loaded *Velociraptor* onto its rack and looked out at the frenzy on the docks, where teams were lining up to put their boats in the water.

Just to the north of the boathouse, along the river, a temporary grandstand had been erected in City Park for the event. It was filled to capacity with fans and spectators. More well-wishers were pressing at the barricades to yell congratulations and watch the crews come off the water.

"I didn't see him — did you?" Nate finally asked, scanning the mass of people. Their father had said he was going to come to the regatta, then celebrate with them afterward. They were supposed to be going into Austin for dinner at Threadgill's and to hear the Lofty Pigs play live. "Was he in the stands?"

"I was concentrating on rowing," Brady replied. "You know, because it was a race."

Nate didn't reply. Neither of them said a word as they headed into the locker room to shower and clean up.

It was supposed to have been only the second time in about seven years that their father emerged from the family ranch. The first time was two months ago, just after the Fourth of July. He'd taken Brady, Nate, and their sister, Ernie, into downtown Bastrop to see *Back to the Future*. To Nate's embarrassment, halfway through, he got them kicked out of the Pegasus Theatre when he started talking loudly and at length about how Dr. Emmett Brown had gotten it all wrong and was a menace. He'd even recited differential equations.

Nate figured he would still be hearing about this from everyone in town five years from now, when he graduated from Bastrop High West and left the state of Texas entirely, for anyplace that hadn't heard of the Chronal Engine, the family time machine.

Their father spent most of his days and nights working on it and obsessing over it.

According to family lore, Nate's Great-Grandpa Pierson, nicknamed "Mad Jack," had invented the Chronal Engine and had used it to defeat the Nazis. Nate wasn't clear on the details of exactly *how* the time machine had won the war, since history books tell the story differently, but the Chronal Engine itself was about the size of a minivan, took up much of the basement, and had lights and dials that sometimes lit up randomly for no reason he could see.

Despite himself, Nate was a little surprised his father wasn't at the regatta. He'd gone out of his way to say he'd come, even though he thought sports were for fools and the people who watched them were ninnies. So on top of being angry at Brady for his performance, Nate was mad at their dad. He was also kind of mad at himself for hoping his father might be starting to let go of the craziness.

Their sister, Ernie, also wasn't there, though, and that was unusual. The three had established a kind of solidarity, supporting one another even if their father didn't, especially since losing their mom in a car accident three years ago. She went to the boys' regattas and recitals and Brady's science fairs, and the twins went to her academic decathlons and track meets. It worked out, mostly, although slightly less regularly now that she'd started dating that idiot Jacob Takahashi. He was on the football team, and Nate really wanted to bludgeon him with an oar.

But apart from the fact that their father had promised he'd be here and wasn't, the boys didn't have a way home.

Nate tried calling their dad using the pay phone in the boathouse, but all he got was the answering machine.

"He's probably on his way," Brady said.

"Right," Nate answered, slamming the receiver down. It was

possible. In the same way it was possible he could win the lottery while getting struck by lightning. Twice.

"He's working," Brady said, as if working on a time machine was perfectly normal.

The pair spent the next couple of hours helping the organizers clean up the boathouse and grounds and prepare for tomorrow. As always, Brady stayed calm while Nate stewed. By sunset, their father still wasn't there and there still wasn't an answer on the home phone.

As Nate hung up, swearing loudly and expressively, Brady reprimanded him for cursing, and the rowing-team coach approached.

"Next time," Coach Halverson said, "maybe your dad can use that time machine of his to pick you up on time." He laughed that hearty and annoying laugh he used to make people think he was joking. "Can I give you kids a lift?"

Brady shrugged. Nate nodded because they didn't really have much of a choice.

The twins were silent most of the way home—Brady didn't really like the coach, and Coach Halverson jabbered enough for three people, anyway. This time, he talked about how in high school the boys' dad used to be normal. Back then, it was their dad's father, Samuel Pierson, who had been the eccentric. Nate grunted in the right places and, every now and then, wiped imaginary dust off his glasses with the end of his T-shirt.

Finally, they got to the ranch, and Coach Halverson turned down the winding, tree-lined road that led up the hill to their house.

Almost before the truck had come to a stop adjacent to the stairs leading to the porch, Nate jumped out and said through clenched teeth, "Thanks!"

Without waiting for Brady, Nate turned and climbed the steps. Coach Halverson waved and spun the wheels and roared off. It actually had been good of the coach to come all the way out here to the ranch, Nate admitted to himself. Of course, that was as much because he wanted the twins (Brady, mostly) on the team next year as anything else. Nate hadn't really needed or wanted to be reminded, though, that their dad was just the latest member of the family to be widely known as the town freak.

Still, Nate figured Mad Jack Pierson must've had something going for him. He was Nate and Brady's great-grandfather and the one who'd bought the three-thousand-acre ranch and built the house in the 1890s. It was a twelve-thousand-square-foot Texas Victorian perched on a hill between Austin and Bastrop and in the shadows of the Lost Pines. It had given him space for his time travel experiments without interference from neighbors, and there was enough land for his own power plant to run the Chronal Engine.

Nate opened the leaded glass door and wiped his feet on the doormat, not bothering to remove his shoes. At that point, he didn't care that if their housekeeper, Frau Lindenhofer, saw him, she'd give him grief about dirt on the hardwood. Of course, it was late enough that she was probably already upstairs, watching the soap operas she recorded every day on videocassette. The front of the house was dark, with only a small table lamp lit in the parlor.

Straight down the hall to the back, behind the closed kitchen door, Nate and Brady heard frantic barking.

"Thor!" Nate yelled, picking up the pace. When he opened the kitchen door, he was nearly bowled over by eighty pounds of golden retriever.

The next few minutes were occupied by the vigorous petting and scratching of dog. Then Nate grabbed a much-slobbered-over plush toy stegosaur from the hallway floor and threw it toward the front. Thor bounded after it, claws clicking and skittering on the wood.

"Dad must be downstairs," Brady observed as Thor returned with his toy. "He told me yesterday he was near a breakthrough with the Recall Device."

Nate rolled his eyes.

According to their dad, the Chronal Engine itself remained fixed in time and space, while the time traveler could operate the machine remotely using these baseball-size things Mad Jack had unimaginatively called Recall Devices. The problem was, it had been years since anyone had seen a Recall Device in the wild. Their father had convinced himself that he could build one, though, and he was perpetually nearing the necessary break-through. But who built any kind of machine that could be oper-ated only from a remote control?

As Nate opened the door, Brady grabbed his arm. "Don't."

Nate shook free and plunged on, stomping down the stairs. The last time he'd been down there, his dad had complained that he'd startled him, ruining three hours of work. Thor raced ahead. Brady followed.

They called the basement "the workshop," but it looked more like a library. The Chronal Engine — lights glowing — occupied one side, and an array of oak bookshelves and file cabinets lined the walls. A burgundy and gold Oriental rug covered the floor. At the far end, French doors opened to the patio, with its barbecue pit and smoker.

Their father was where he usually was, at the library desk, which was about the size of an aircraft carrier. A pile of tiny parts and a set of watchmaker's tools were arranged in front of him on the blotter. He wore a jeweler's loupe over his right eye and held a tiny screwdriver in one hand and, in the other, a small round object made of glass and brass. A fine-tip soldering iron sat next to him on the desktop.

Thor ran between the red leather armchairs to push his head forward on the desk.

"Get that dog out of here!" their father said without looking up.

"We were supposed to go to Threadgill's!" Nate approached to rest a hand on the back of one of the chairs.

"You're already home," their father replied, making an adjustment with the screwdriver. "Therefore, to drive into Austin would've been a waste. And you know better than to bring that animal in here!"

"The regatta ended hours ago!" Nate shouted.

At this, his father looked up at him, the loupe reflecting the lights from the Chronal Engine. "Impossible!"

"It's dark out! Look!" Nate pointed toward the French doors.

His father glanced over, momentarily startled, and seemed about to say something. But then Thor plopped his head, tongue lolling out, onto a small pile of tiny spare cogs and gears. At least, Nate thought they were spare. His father recoiled and yelled, with emphasis on every word, "Get him out of here now!"

Thor wagged his tail and barked, running toward the patio through the open doors.

Nate's father peered down at the pile the dog had disturbed, then looked over the edge of the desk to see where parts were now scattered on the floor.

Nate clenched his jaw and, like Frau Lindenhofer always recommended, counted silently to ten in German before he said something regrettable. Then he shook his head and followed Thor, wanting more than anything to just get out of the house. Besides, there'd been a couple of reports recently of coyotes and Nate didn't want to leave Thor outside alone.

Brady caught up with him as Nate stepped onto the patio. Back in the workshop, their dad was on his hands and knees, picking up tiny pieces.

"He always does it," Nate said.

That was when they heard barking from down the hill near the garage.

"He's got something," Brady murmured, and raced ahead.

The garage had been built in the 1930s and was two stories tall, with a yellow-brick face and a red tile roof. As Nate ran after his brother, he could see that the side door was open.

Thor had already pushed his way through and disappeared into the interior. Nate flicked on the lights and hit the buttons that opened the doors to the three bays. Only two were occupied now.

"You don't think he caught anything, do you?" Brady asked as they entered and circled around a station wagon.

"Oh yeah," Nate muttered. "He brought down a caribou." Thor was a good dog—mostly obedient and loudly aware of strange noises in the night. This had been useful when Nate was five and was scared of the bogeyman and Sasquatch. Now Thor's barking in the middle of the night wasn't so great. And Nate had never, ever seen him catch anything.

The first bay in the garage held the station wagon. A blue '75 Chevy Bel Air with the 454-cubic-inch V8 because their dad didn't believe in four-cylinder engines. The middle bay was empty, and the third, where they could hear Thor, was occupied by Dad's bass boat on its trailer.

The boat was top of the line and had been used maybe once. About twenty feet long, with a row of three bucket seats in the middle, the rightmost one behind the control console and dashboard. Behind the row of seats were a raised fishing chair and the outboard motor. In front of the cockpit was a flat deck with storage compartments beneath it and another fishing chair. Stowed at the bow was a small electric trolling motor.

Along the far wall of the garage, past the bass boat, was a tool cabinet and mini-fridge. At the wall's base, where the floor trim was brittle with dry rot, Thor was scratching away plaster and wood lath. Nate raced over and grabbed him by the collar, pulling him back. Then he peered into the hole the dog had uncovered. A small brown and white shape sprang out and raced across the garage floor. Both Brady and Nate jumped back, and Thor lunged after it, chasing it out through an open bay door.

"Rabbit," Brady said. "Harmless. It'll get away."

"Thor!" Nate shouted. Then he spotted something in the hole. He pulled away a bit more of the wood and plaster to reveal an object nestled in the back.

It was a dusty brass and glass sphere. Nate swore in disbelief.

This time in German, which Frau Lindenhofer had also taught him how to do.

"It's a Recall Device," Brady said, leaning in.

"I know." Nate reached in, pulled it out through the hole, and stood, blowing away dust.

Brady turned away, sneezing. "How long do you think it's been in there?"

"A while." Though the cloud was dissipating, the glass and brass ball was still coated with a layer of grime.

"Dad is going to freak out," Brady said.

"If we tell him," Nate replied, only half serious, though still angry about this afternoon.

Nate licked his thumb and rubbed at the top of the Device to clean it off.

"No, don't!"

Nate felt a click as something shifted. There was a brief moment of nothing and then a flash of light.

MAX
PRESENT DAY

I WAS DREAMING. I KNEW I WAS DREAMING, BUT I COULDN'T STOP it. I was in a VW Beetle and my brother, Kyle, was driving and our friend Petra was in the back seat. We were caught in a stampede of *Parasaurolophus* and were pushed over a cliff. Then we were falling toward something that had no bottom, and that's when I woke up.

"Max!" My sister, Emma, came down the basement stairs, pausing at the bottom. She was barefoot, wearing jeans and a University of Texas T-shirt, hair in a clip, and looked more composed than anyone should that early in the morning. "You okay? You were dreaming."

"I know," I told her, blinking and suppressing a groan. I'd fallen asleep sitting cross-legged on the rug on the concrete floor of my grandfather's workshop, leaning back against a file cabinet. Assorted folders and books surrounded me.

"Here." Emma held out a mug. "Coffee. It'll stunt your growth. With half-and-half and two teaspoons of sugar. Just the way you like it."

"Good. Thanks." I stood and gestured toward a stack of books. "Don't knock that over."

Emma, Kyle, and I were staying with Grandpa Pierson in the Victorian mansion on the family ranch while Mom was on a paleontology dig in Mongolia. At the moment, though, we were sort of on our own, since Grandpa was in the hospital in Austin and Mrs. Castillo, his nurse, cook, assistant, and all-around manager, was there with him.

I took the coffee as I stepped around the stack I'd warned Emma about. Then, as we sat in the red leather chairs facing the desk, she asked, "What were you dreaming about?"

For a moment after I told her, she just looked at me over the top of her mug. "In the past week, you were nearly eaten by a *T. rex*—twice—and you're telling me the thing that scared you so much that you have nightmares about it was the car accident?"

We—Emma, Kyle, Petra, and I—had spent the past week or so about seventy million years ago in Late Cretaceous Texas, after Emma had been kidnapped by this guy named Isambard Campbell, an ex-colleague of our great-great-grandfather "Mad Jack" Pierson. Campbell apparently wanted to get his hands on our great-great-grandpa's Chronal Engine, the time machine that still occupied a corner of the workshop.

I shrugged. "It happened." But in real life the car had fallen into a river, not a bottomless pit. "Besides, what's more likely? Being in a car accident or getting eaten by a *T. rex*?"

"In our family?" Emma rolled her eyes, then gestured with her mug. "What's all this?" She looked around, taking in the open file drawers and the collection of watchmaker's tools, the Recall Device, and odd components lying on the desk blotter. "I'd've thought you'd want to sleep in a real bed, first day back from the Cretaceous and all."

We'd gotten back to the ranch yesterday afternoon. We'd actually been gone only about an hour in our time, which meant that no one had really noticed we were missing. We had had to drop Kyle off at St. Joseph's Hospital in Bastrop — he'd been mauled by a *Nanotyrannus*. (We told the people at the hospital that it had been a black bear outside the state park — which, granted, was a little unusual for central Texas, but they seemed to have bought it.)

So, last night, I'd had my first hot shower in days and a dinner of leftover fried chicken. Afterward, when Emma had gone up to her room to sleep in what she called "regal comfort" (by which she mostly meant "air-conditioned"), I'd come down here to the also-air-conditioned basement workshop/library to try to sort out more of the family history and how the Chronal Engine actually worked.

"Research," I told Emma. I took a sip of the coffee, then made a face. Even with the half-and-half and two sugars, the stuff always smelled better than it tasted. I took another sip and gestured at the leather case sitting next to a Recall Device on the desk. "The time-space crystal things."

"Chronally resonant crystals" was their technical name. These were apparently the key to the Recall Devices, which used them to sync up somehow with the Chronal Engine so that the bearer could travel through time. They were kind of fragile, though, and didn't always work. And I was having trouble figuring out how the things actually fit into a Recall Device.

"Did you learn anything?"

"Not really." I yawned.

My sister stood. "Come on. I told Petra to come over." She led the way out the French doors to the patio.

When we sat down on the rattan chairs, Petra was already striding up the walkway from the house on the property she shared with her mother, Mrs. Castillo. Petra was my age — a year younger than Kyle and Emma — going into eighth grade, and kind of outdoorsy, which had been useful back in the Age of Dinosaurs. She knew her way around a bow and arrow and could also field dress and butcher game animals of varying sizes. About my height, she had black hair and dark green eyes. She wore hiking boots, brown shorts, and a denim shirt with epaulets. On one leg was a discreet brace for a sprained ankle, and she had a cut over her eye.

She also seemed to have a soft spot for things that were small and cute, like the down-covered baby dromaeosaur chick that rested on one of the epaulets like a pirate's parrot. She'd found Aki in the Cretaceous, and the creature had apparently imprinted, much like a baby duck bonding with its mother.

I wasn't sure it was a good idea in terms of the space-time continuum to bring Aki back with us, but just leaving him behind to get eaten by a predator or accidentally stomped on by a giant sauropod seemed cruel. Also, it would be a while before he got big and his sickle claw grew out and he tried to disembowel us.

"Still planning on teaching him to hunt?" Emma asked as Petra came into earshot. Petra had this idea of training Aki like falconers do with, well, falcons. I supposed it was possible — he wouldn't grow up to be too much bigger than a golden eagle, and I'd seen this YouTube video of some girl in Mongolia who had trained one of those.

Petra scratched the dromaeosaur under the chin. "I think I'll wait until he gets his real feathers." She grinned. "I let him down by the henhouse. He went after the chicks. I had to rescue him from the rooster."

As Emma snorted into her mug, we were all startled by a booming sound from down the hill near the garage, which housed Grandpa's bass boat and Hummer. It also used to be home to the VW Beetle we'd left in the river back in the Cretaceous. Aki spread his feathered arms and hissed.

"Please tell me that was thunder," Emma said.

"It was thunder," I answered as a pair of figures emerged from around one of the live oaks that shaded the patio.

"Is that any way to greet your big brother?" the closer of the two demanded.

"Kyle!" Emma shouted, and sprang forward to grip her twin in a fierce hug. Then she stepped back. "Why aren't you in the hospital? Where are your bandages? And I swear you're an inch taller."

"Bigger, too," Petra noted.

I didn't reply. But they were both right. Carrying a black backpack, and wearing a tank top and shiny black basketball shorts, he did look like he'd spent more time lifting weights.

Kyle grinned and gestured at the figure next to him. "I've been living with Uncle Nate for the past six months. Seeing the sights." He flexed his biceps. "Working out."

"You know about the Chronal Engine?" Emma asked our uncle. "I mean, duh, you know, but how long have you known that it works?"

"A while," Uncle Nate answered, adjusting his glasses.

"And Kyle's been with you in London for six months?" I asked, just as surprised as Emma.

Our uncle, who was a couple of years younger than Mom, was some kind of physicist and spent a lot of time in Europe, so we didn't see him much.

He stepped forward to hug Emma and me. After we introduced him to Petra, we all sat down in the outdoor seating area.

"So what happened?" I asked calmly, although I was a little weirded out that Kyle was now six months older. He'd always been kind of annoying about being the oldest (older than Emma by about ten minutes), so this was definitely not going to help. Okay, I was a lot weirded out.

Uncle Nate held up a Recall Device. "I checked your brother out of the hospital a few minutes after you guys left and took him back with me."

"Why?" I asked, leaning forward, still digesting the news that Uncle Nate not only knew about Recall Devices but had been using one. I wondered if our mom knew.

"A couple reasons," Uncle Nate answered, looking directly at me. "First, there were things he needed to know. Second, there were the preventive rabies shots. Third, I need you to return to the Cretaceous, find me, and help me get back here. To 1985, actually."

There was a moment of silence.

"You, meaning me?" I swallowed. "And me, meaning you?"

"You" — Kyle pointed — "meaning you and Petra. And him, but younger him."

Now Petra looked startled. "Not you or Emma?"

Kyle shook his head.

"I can't tell you a lot," Uncle Nate said, holding up his hand. "I don't *think* you'll change the past by knowing what you're going to do or have done, but the solutions to the multidimensional temporal-spatial equations are slightly ambiguous, so that's still a possibility. The less you know, the better."

"Equations?" Petra asked.

"Uncle Nate does time travel research," Kyle said.

"Is there anyone in your family who doesn't?" she replied.

"Uncle Nate has a PhD in physics, though," I said. From what I had been able to glean, back in the day, Mad Jack Pierson had been self-taught and an excellent engineer as well as theoretician but had had issues with just about everyone who wasn't him. A century later, Uncle Nate worked at Princeton and CERN. If nothing else, he had credentials. "Can you tell us *why* you want us to go?"

Uncle Nate nodded. "Thirty years ago, when I was your age, I inadvertently went back to the Cretaceous . . . and you and Petra . . . appeared there as well. With the little dromaeosaur, too, I might add. I probably shouldn't tell you anything else." Then he hesitated. "But Kyle has supplies that should be adequate."

Kyle tossed the backpack at my feet. I unzipped the main body to find a pair of canteens with a packet of water purification tablets, a half-dozen energy bars, a couple of hunting knives, matches in a resealable plastic bag, a polyester first-aid pouch, and a flint and steel. In an outside pocket was a compass.

"You'll want to pack a change of clothing, too," Uncle Nate said.

It wasn't a lot. It was insanely little, in fact, to be taking to a place where the small predators were the size of grizzly bears. "Can I take an elephant gun this time?"

Uncle Nate shook his head. "No. For one thing, you don't

know how to use an elephant gun. For another, Petra can take her compound bow."

It was not all that reassuring. Although, honestly, the bow had been enough last time. Barely. "Where are Emma and Kyle going to be?"

"They're coming with me," Uncle Nate said, "to Mad Jack Pierson's time, just before he completes his work on the Chronal Engine."

"We are?" Emma said, staring first at Kyle, then at our uncle. "Why?"

"What happens if we decide *not* to go back?" Petra put in before Kyle or Uncle Nate could answer. "Do we change the future? In the past?"

"You could," my uncle replied, "if you stick by that decision and don't unmake it." He didn't look that concerned, though. "But if you do, the entire argument is moot."

"But you're here, so regardless, we've succeeded in bringing you back." I leaned back, steepling my fingers, trying to appear confident.

"Maybe," Uncle Nate answered. "As I said, the equations are slightly ambiguous. But I do think there has to be room for free will, so not everything is written in stone. Maybe not anything." He stood. "Look, I know this is a lot to ask, so I'll give you guys a few minutes to talk it over." With that, he went inside to the workshop.

I let out a breath and leaned back in my chair, staring while the French doors closed behind him. Then, nodding at Petra, I asked, "What do you think?"

She ran a finger down Aki's back before replying. "We take the Recall Device, go back, find him, and then come back here. Easy-peasy."

Emma turned to our brother. "And why would *we* want to go back to the twentieth century?"

Kyle squirmed under her stare. "We have to talk to Mad Jack. And Samuel."

"Samuel?" I blurted. Samuel was Mad Jack Pierson's son and our great-grandfather, whom we had met when we were trying to find Emma. He'd been there looking for Mad Jack. "So he found his father?"

"I guess," Kyle answered, still looking uncomfortable. I couldn't tell if he knew and didn't want to say or if he didn't know and didn't want to admit it.

The last time we'd seen Samuel, he had taken off on a river launch — a steamboat — that had once belonged to his father. The problem, and I don't think we told him, was that when we'd arrived in the Cretaceous, we'd found a burned-out river launch identical to his but that seemed to be from a different time. We still didn't know how — or when — it had gotten there.

"Um, Max, you haven't said what you think," Petra said.

I hesitated. I didn't like the idea. But. "I think I have to go. And go prepared." I glanced toward the French doors and leaned forward. Before he'd moved to England, Uncle Nate had always been, well, normal and aboveboard with us. And he gave great Christmas and birthday presents. If he said this was something we needed to do, then I guess it was. "I think we're tied up in this, but I don't think you are." Petra was a friend, and kind of awesome in every way, but this wasn't her problem. I had a sudden feeling of déjà vu, like before our last adventure. "You don't have to go."

She lifted Aki off her shoulder and onto her index finger. The dromaeosaur chick squeaked. "It'll be fun."

We didn't tell Uncle Nate that, exactly, in part because I wasn't sure if Petra was serious or not. But when he came out of the workshop, he was holding the Recall Device from the desk.

"I installed the crystals," he said, then tossed the sphere to me.

I had a brief flash of panic but managed to catch the thing without breaking it or looking too ridiculous. I'd never claimed to have great hand-eye coordination. I ignored Kyle's snort.

Fifteen minutes later, after we grabbed Petra's bow and arrows and a change of clothing each, we were back on the patio. I hoisted the backpack over both shoulders and attached a hunting knife to my belt.

"And remember," Uncle Nate said, wagging his finger, "play nice."

"We'll be back in time for dinner," I replied as I pressed the button on the Recall Device.

I wasn't sure, but just before the flash of light, I thought I heard Uncle Nate say, "Not for your next one, you won't."

CHAPTER

III

NATE

AN INSTANT LATER, **N**ATE WAS IN OPEN AIR, AN EXPANSE OF WATER about three feet below.

Both he and Brady yelled as they splashed down. At the same time, to their right, the bass boat, complete with its trailer, crashed into the surface, swamping them with its impact wave.

Nate kicked up, holding his glasses in place with one hand and clutching the Recall Device with the other. "It works!" he shouted to his brother when Brady emerged beside him. "I can't believe it! The Chronal Engine actually works!" Treading water, Nate spun in a circle, trying to get a feel for where they were, catching a glimpse of a tree-lined shore, maybe fifty yards off.

"Get us out of here!" Brady yelled.

Nate peered closely at the object in his hand, the water on his glasses blurring his vision. The Recall Device had dials and markings that made it look like a slide rule version of the clouds on Jupiter. From what his father had said, you were supposed to use it to set destination times and dates and places. Once activated, it communicated with the Chronal Engine, which actually did the transmitting to convey the traveler. Like a client terminal and a mainframe. But Nate had no idea how to actually operate the Device. It was a lot more complicated than a VCR or microwave oven. "We could end up in a volcano!"

Brady shook his hair out of his face and frowned. "Yeah, maybe. Let's get out of the water and then figure it out."

That was when Nate noticed the bow of the boat was tilting down, the trailer dragging it under by the winch cable.

He swam to the front of the boat and tried to unlock the catch, but there wasn't enough slack.

"Here," Brady said as he reached around and released the catch-piece tab that blocked the crank.

Before Nate could move, the handle began spinning and rammed into the hand that held the Recall Device.

"No!" Nate exclaimed as the Device shot from his grip and into the water. He grabbed for it but couldn't reach it before it sank out of sight.

"Get it!" Brady yelled unhelpfully from the other side of the trailer, which was now sinking as the cable unwound.

In a panic, Nate dived down to look. He couldn't see anything through the sting of the water and the silt, though, and his ears felt the pressure of the depth before he felt bottom.

When he surfaced, he saw Brady release the cable winch, and the boat bobbed free. Then Brady turned to Nate. "Find it!"

Although Nate couldn't see the bottom, or how deep the water really was, it seemed they were in the middle of a swampy, irregularly shaped lagoon, part of a larger lake, not that far from shore. Around them, what looked like cypresses and ferns lined the banks. It couldn't be that deep, he figured.

"Where were you when you dropped it?" Brady asked, right before disappearing under the water.

Nate dived again, struck his head against something, and recoiled. Surfacing, he coughed water.

Brady popped up beside him, holding his forehead. "Watch where you're going."

Brady dived back down, while Nate took off his gym shoes and tossed them onto the bow of the boat. Then he dived again too, holding his glasses in place with one hand. The water was still too murky to see anything beyond a few feet. Reaching out, he felt for the trailer but didn't find anything before he needed air.

Brady popped to the surface beside him. "Nothing!"

That's when Nate felt something slip by him in the water, nudging his leg. And then another. And another. They were about ten feet long and kind of sinewy, like big lizards. And when the creatures broke the surface to breathe, Nate could make out long, huge mouths filled with many, many sharp teeth. "Sea serpents! Get out of the water!"

Brady pulled himself up onto the bow of the boat first. As

something enormous breached the surface of the water, Nate grabbed on to Brady's outstretched arm and practically leaped upward right as another something latched on to his right leg, just above the knee. Nate screamed.

"Hang on!" Brady yelled as Nate felt his grip slipping. He looked down — his leg was caught in the creature's mouth. Frantically, he kicked with his free foot against the sea serpent's hard skull. Then he felt his heel hit something soft and the animal released him.

With a yank, Brady pulled Nate onto the front deck of the boat.

Breathing heavily, and shivering despite the heat, Nate looked over the side of the boat. The creatures were swimming off toward a large channel bracketed by trees and ferns.

"Mosasaurs," Brady said. "But they shouldn't be here."

"Yeah, well, neither should we," Nate told his brother, then tried to stand. Wincing at the pain in his leg, eyes watering, he sat on the fishing chair, rolled up his pant leg, and looked at the wound.

It was bleeding from five or six punctures, blood oozing over the knee and then down his calf. His leg really hurt.

As his brother rifled through a glove compartment in the cockpit, Nate asked, like he'd asked him many times before just to give him grief, "Why do you even know that? And, oh, by the way: Where and when are we?"

Everyone in the family had gone through a dinosaur phase,

in part because of the fossil dinosaur tracks on the ranch down by Little Buddy Creek. Nate had never been all that into it, but Ernie had gobbled up every book and videotape on dinosaurs she could find, and Brady did too. He'd even gone to a lecture in Austin by a paleontologist named Bakker who said that dinosaurs might be warm-blooded and some could even have had feathers. And that *birds* were their descendants.

Brady snorted and handed Nate a red first-aid kit from a shelf in the boat's cockpit. "There should be some antiseptic in here."

Using the scissors from the kit, Nate cut the legs of his jeans off just above the knees. With a gauze pad, he applied hydrogen peroxide to the wounds. Then he taped the pads over the bite marks, using up the entire supply. To take his mind off the sting, he asked, "What do you mean, they shouldn't be here? And what's a mosasaur?"

Shielding his eyes from the sun, Brady peered out over the lake. "They're sort of like aquatic Komodo dragons, but bigger. I'm sure you already figured out that part. But they're not known from freshwater environments."

"Wonderful," Nate replied. He stood and limped toward the cockpit and lowered himself into the driver's seat. Then he saw the look on his brother's face. "And?"

Brady hesitated. "And the bite of the Komodo dragon might be dangerous, so it's possible the bites of mosasaurs are too. If they're anything like Komodo dragons, they probably aren't going to have poison of their own, but their teeth might collect all kinds of funky bacteria, which can cause really bad infections in their prey."

"So you're saying I probably need an antivenin or something," Nate said, frowning and trying to restrain the need to pummel something. Or someone.

"An antibiotic," Brady replied. "I think infection is probably the biggest risk."

"Terrific," Nate muttered. "And the only way we have to get back home is the Recall Device, which is now at the bottom of a moat guarded by the same poisonous sea serpents."

Brady was silent a moment. "There's some kind of primitive cathode ray tube video screen on the Chronal Engine. I think it can be used to track Recall Devices. Maybe Dad will notice we're gone and check it out."

"Dad?" Nate asked. "Notice we're gone? Really?"

"Yeah, okay."

"And if he does notice and can track us, then shouldn't he appear, like, right now?" Nate gestured like he was a magician. Nothing happened. "Or assuming we do get back, what's to stop us from sending someone here now to bring us back earlier?"

Again, nothing happened.

"We're on our own, then," Brady said.

MAX

WE MATERIALIZED IN FAMILIAR TERRITORY. OR AT LEAST, FAMILIAR to me. Mad Jack Pierson had built himself a Cretaceous getaway — a traditional Texas dogtrot on an island on a picturesque lake — which I'd visited once before. Basically consisting of a pair of two-room cottages with a shared roof and separated by the dogtrot breezeway, it had most of the hallmarks of an early-twentieth-century home, including electricity, but not, unfortunately, air conditioning or indoor plumbing.

We landed on the small wooden pier where Mad Jack Pierson used to tie up his boat. It was hot and humid, just like I'd remembered. And there were deadly things in the forest.

"Why did Mad Jack build this?" Petra asked, glancing around.

I shrugged my shoulders. He had liked dinosaurs. Almost everyone in the family did. "So far as I know, he just wanted to get away from it all."

"No," she said. "I get that. What I want to know is, why *here?*

And how?" She gestured at the island, the lake, and the forest on the shore a hundred yards away.

"Safety?" I answered, and it sounded more like a question than I'd intended.

"Dinosaurs don't swim?"

"They do," I said. "Probably, but I doubt they'd come out here without a good reason. There's at least one study saying sauropods would have been too top-heavy and would have sort of tipped over. But there's not really anything they would want to eat here, anyway. And where there's no prey, there are no predators." I sighed. "As to how, I think he must've used the steamboat, or the Recall Device built into it, to bring all the materials."

I led the way onto the island and up the stairs going to the cottages. They looked identical to the way I'd seen them last.

"Hmm," Petra said, looking around more. "I guess that sort of makes sense. But isn't Nate supposed to be here?"

Cupping my hands to my mouth, I shouted, "Hello! Anyone there?"

As we walked up to the breezeway, Petra suddenly stopped beside me and pointed. "What are those?"

Between the island and the shoreline, not far from where the lake emptied into a river, a pair of pterosaurs had landed. Big ones. Standing upright on all four legs, they were tall, almost as tall as giraffes. They waded through the water, then peered down and suddenly snatched their heads back up, fish wriggling in their five-foot-long mouths.

"*Quetzalcoatlus*," I said. "I saw some last time." They were amazing, like real-life dragons. I liked them better now that they were farther away.

We made our way into the breezeway. It needed sweeping, but there was no other evidence of disuse or lack of habitation.

Four doors opened onto the passageway. On one side was a workshop and kitchen. On the other was a pair of bedrooms.

"What's the setting on the Recall Device?" Petra asked.

I shook my head. "It doesn't matter. It got us to where we're supposed to be."

The workshop was as I remembered it. Tools were displayed on a pegboard along one wall. A ceiling fan wasn't moving. When I pulled the chain, the lights didn't go on.

I set the Recall Device down on the workbench, dumped my backpack beside it, and opened the fuse box. None of the fuses looked like they'd blown.

"There's a generator outside," I said, peering through a window to a shed out back, next to an outhouse. "Maybe it ran out of gas."

I followed Petra into the kitchen. A wood stove occupied one corner, with a cast-iron teakettle resting on top. A farmhouse sink sat under a window, and a butcher-block prep table occupied the center of the room. A table with two chairs sat next to it. Petra placed her bow on top of it and began opening cabinet doors.

Cans of food were stored in a cupboard along the wall opposite the sink. Peas. Corn. Beans. Campbell's soup.

"Flour and sugar here too," Petra observed, peering into a pair of canisters. Aki hopped from her shoulder and looked in, sneezing as a cloud of flour rose from the larger of the two.

"He lived here for a while," I said. "Mad Jack, I mean."

"Why did he leave?" she asked.

I shrugged. "Maybe someone found him. Or he ran away so no one would."

I stared out the window over the sink. Across the channel, a group of ostrich-like ornithomimosaurs approached the water and began to drink. Farther away, the *Quetzalcoatlus* ignored them.

As I turned to speak to Petra, a loud rumble came from the next room and the entire cottage shook. A moment later, there was another rumble.

"What was that?" Petra asked, holding out a hand to comfort a now-cowering Aki.

I raced to the door and into the workshop. The two windows had been blown out and the ceiling fan was spinning slowly.

"Oh no." The Recall Device wasn't on the workbench. I crouched, checking to see if it had rolled onto the floor. It hadn't.

"What are you . . . oh," Petra said.

"Someone took it," I mumbled. "Someone was here, watching us . . ."

"You put it down?" she said, eyes growing wider. "Why?"

My face went red. "I was looking for Nate and anything that could help us find him!" I exclaimed.

She rubbed the cut over her eye. "Did your uncle know this was going to happen?" Petra asked. "And who took it?"

"I don't know," I answered. "That's the problem. It could be anyone."

"But who knew we were going to be here?" Petra persisted. "Your uncle. Your brother and sister. No one else."

"Unless we make it back and tell someone," I replied. "Unless they told someone we were going to be here when they went back in time."

"So it really could be anyone," she said.

"Yes," I told her. "But, then, someone should have come for us, you know, when we don't show up on time. Didn't. Whatever."

"Unless they don't know we didn't make it back because —"

"Because they don't make it back either."

CHAPTER
V

NATE

NATE POPPED A COUPLE OF ASPIRIN FROM THE FIRST-AID KIT. HOW long, he wondered, did it take to die of blood poisoning or gangrene?

He was not, he decided, going to wait and find out.

"Drop the anchor," he told his brother, and stood, pulling off his T-shirt. "I'm going to find the Recall Device."

"Are you dense?" Brady exclaimed. "The mosasaurs are still out there! Look!" He pointed in the direction the creatures had gone. At first, Nate saw nothing, but then one of the mosasaurs surfaced for air, then another. "I'm pretty sure they can smell blood, too!"

"Then what do we do?" Nate asked, grinding his teeth in frustration.

Brady used his hand to shield his eyes from the sun and pointed to a channel, away from the mosasaurs and flanked by clusters of cypresses and ferns. "First, let's get off the open water. Maybe there'll be more shade."

Nate turned the ignition key and said a silent prayer of thanks that the engine hadn't been damaged by its drop into the lagoon.

Then he adjusted the throttle lever, steering toward the channel mouth. The sun beat down from a nearly cloudless sky. To Nate it felt and smelled sort of like Houston in the summer—fetid and humid, with the occasional whiff of dead fish. In the distance, he could hear birds and insects screeching.

A shadow passed over, and Nate flinched while his twin looked up and whistled.

"This is incredible!" Brady said, staring. "Do you know how incredible this is?"

"I get it," Nate told him. But his brother wasn't the one sitting here with holes in his leg. "What kind of dinosaur is it, and is it going to eat us?"

"*Quetzalcoatlus*, I'd guess, judging from the size and proportion of the wings. And pterosaurs aren't dinosaurs." He watched as the pterosaur soared overhead, circled twice, then flew off. "They're archosaurs, like crocodiles."

Nate had no idea what that meant, so he decided to change the subject. "Is there another way we could signal to Dad?"

"What do you think?"

Nate nodded. He hadn't really had much hope. He felt like throwing up.

When he was six, when his mom was still alive, they'd taken a really long road trip out to see the McDonald Observatory in far west Texas.

The landscape was barren as far as the eye could see. His

family hadn't seen another car in hours, and Nate remembered thinking that they were the most alone people in the world. They drove late into the night, and when he got out of the station wagon at the campsite, he fell on his face, dizzy with vertigo because the stars and the moon were so very much there, right on top of them. He'd felt really, really small.

This was orders of magnitude worse. Nate's face suddenly felt unimaginably warm, and everything in front of him went bright.

The next thing he knew, he was lying on his back and his face was wet.

"You okay?" Brady asked, leaning over him, shielding the sun.

Nate squinted and sat up. "Yeah. It just felt as if we were at the bottom of a hole that was, like, light-years deep."

"Try not to fall overboard next time."

"What?"

"Kidding," Brady said, helping Nate back up into the driver's seat.

"I could use some water."

Brady handed Nate a canteen and shook it. "It's warm but clean. I found some water purification tablets."

Nate took a sip and nearly gagged. It was more than just a little warm. Then he noticed a compartment open at the front of the boat. "What's there?"

"Take a look."

Nate stood, a little wobbly, leg throbbing, and stepped

forward. The compartment housed fishing gear, including a pair of rods and reels, a tackle box, and a bait bucket. When he opened the tackle box, he found a filet knife, extra line, and fishhooks and sinkers. "Just normal fishing stuff."

"I guess it's here if we have to use it," Brady said. "To fish, I mean. Assuming we even should."

"What?"

"What if by fishing we change the time stream? Like in *Back to the Future*, only worse?"

Nate hesitated, crouching by the next compartment. "That can't be right. Because the time machine exists and it's been used, and the future hasn't been changed."

"But it could be that we wouldn't know because we'd be changed with it," Brady said.

Nate nodded. That's what their dad had said way back at the Pegasus Theatre.

"But if we don't know, would it matter?" Nate asked, swatting at a swarm of gnats.

Brady had a point. They didn't know, really. But Nate did know that he was not going to sit around and do nothing on the off chance that doing something could affect the time stream. Just sitting around doing nothing could affect the time stream in an even worse way, for all they knew.

"All right, then, if I wake up tomorrow and you're gone, it's not my fault." Brady held up a machete and a hunting knife, both in leather scabbards. "I also found these."

Nate grinned despite himself. He attached the hunting knife to his belt and sat, crossing his good leg under himself on the boat's deck next to the front fishing seat. "Do you know where we are, exactly?"

"Late Cretaceous Texas," Brady replied, "judging from the *Quetzalcoatlus* and the mosasaur. I haven't seen enough of the rest of the flora and fauna to know for sure."

To Nate, his brother may as well have been speaking in Farsi. "Does that mean we're going to see a *Brontosaurus* or a *Tyrannosaurus rex* anytime soon?"

"*Apatosaurus*," he replied. "*Brontosaurus* is . . . never mind. And they didn't coexist. *T. rex* is closer in time to us than to *Apatosaurus*. And if we're in the latest Cretaceous, then yes, we might see a *T. rex*."

"Really?" Nate exclaimed. "That's so cool!"

His brother gave him a wry look. "Except that they have teeth the size of bananas and are big enough to swallow you whole."

When he put it that way, it didn't sound nearly as much fun.

With that, Brady took his turn behind the boat's steering wheel and guided them toward the channel. Nate glanced down into the water. Although it was still on the murky side, he could now see fish. Big fish—like, a couple of feet long. Silver, with red flecks along their sides. They were all going in the opposite direction the boat was heading. The really distinctive thing about them, though, was the three-inch fangs.

"Huh," Nate said.

"What?" Brady asked, peering down.

"Fish. Like vampire trout."

"Saber-toothed herrings," Brady answered. "*Enchodus*. They're not really herrings. They're actually more closely related to salmon."

"Why do they need three-inch fangs?" Nate asked.

"To suck your blood."

The air was oppressively thick, and it seemed to get even worse as the channel grew narrower and the ferns and cycads grew closer. The sky was growing cloudy too, but if the times Nate had gone to present-day Galveston were any indication, rain wouldn't help with the humidity.

He climbed over the seats to check out the compartments in the rear of the boat. One was an empty but big live well to store a catch. Stowed by its side were a landing net and another bait bucket. The last compartment held a hibachi grill, a box of matches in a plastic bag, a flint and steel, and a BIC lighter.

Gradually, the tree ferns gave way to a clearer channel, with more cypress trees growing into the water, their root knees sticking above the surface like weird periscopes.

Occasionally, Nate peered over the side to watch the *Enchodus* swim.

The boys seemed to have an adequate supply of water and Nate figured they wouldn't have too much trouble building a shelter. That he knew how to do from summer camp. And as for food . . .

He grabbed the landing net and went to stand at the bow of the boat.

"Don't fall in," Brady said.

"Slow down a little," Nate told him, gesturing with the long-handled net.

Brady adjusted the throttle to idle. For a moment, they drifted. Then Nate lowered the net, swinging it through the water with both hands on the handle. When he heaved it back up, three fish were caught.

It was more than enough for today, although Nate was really hungry since he'd missed dinner back home. But catching the fish gave him something to do other than think about his throbbing leg and the fact that they were the only humans on the planet. He stowed the fish in the live well, stashed the net and sat down on the fishing chair at the bow of the boat.

The channel grew steadily narrower again, the waterway was only about five or so feet wide. Nate was beginning to think they'd have to turn around when they came to a bend.

And right after the bend, standing on a fallen tree that bridged the channel, was a girl.

MAX

P ETRA AND I EXPLORED THE CABIN FURTHER BUT DIDN'T FIND ANY-thing particularly worthwhile. At least, not if our goal was to get home. There was a linen cabinet in each of the bedrooms, made of cedar, according to Petra, which was supposed to prevent moths. There was no evidence of mice because mice wouldn't evolve for another twenty million years or so.

Out back was a different story. In a side building stood an oil-burning generator and a really big tank beside it.

Petra looked at the generator. "Just needs some fuel." She checked some hoses, then adjusted a spigot. "There." After a moment, the generator began spinning and the light bulb hanging overhead sputtered into light.

"Umm, how did you know how to do that?" I asked.

"Your grandfather has the same one on the ranch," she replied. "To operate the Chronal Engine."

I nodded. I guess that meant that, back in the day, Mad Jack Pierson had probably bought two for the price of one. Or something like that.

The island wasn't large. Maybe about five or six times the area of the dogtrot and the generator hut. A trio of cypress trees anchored one end of the island, at the edge of a wet stand of horsetails. We circled the hut, past a ginkgo tree, ending up at a marsh.

"Look," Petra said, walking to an overturned canoe. A pair of paddles were leaning against one of the cypresses. "It's new. Hasn't been here long. The lacquer's not faded."

I shook my head, not sure what to make of it. We headed back into the dogtrot and sat on the Adirondack chairs in the passageway. With the lights up and running, and the prevailing wind and ceiling fans providing some relief from the heat, it was actually kind of nice. I started thinking.

From the last time we had been here, I knew the geography. Sort of. To our south, a river ran out of the lake to the shore of the Western Interior Seaway. Along the banks of the river was a forest of redwoods, like the trees you'd see in Northern California. But to get there, you had to pass through a hilly region. We could see the tallest hill from the cabin. And from there we'd have a panoramic view of the river and lake country. We'd be able to see signs of smoke from fires or even a boat on this river.

The problem was, it was a good four or five hours' walk away. Through territory teeming with large predators in the tyrannosaur family.

I didn't like the fact that we didn't have an easy way back

home. And that there was someone now who knew we were here and had stolen our Recall Device.

But the cabin didn't seem to contain any more useful information, although it had all kinds of stuff that would help if we wanted to stick around here for a while.

It definitely seemed that our arrival now was *after* our visit the last time, when Campbell was holding Emma hostage here. To me and Petra, it had been just a couple of days. In this time, it could've been a lot longer. But that still meant that downriver, on the shore of the Western Interior Seaway, was a half-sunken steamboat. Which had, at one point, a functioning Recall Device. Built in. Which we might be able to use to get home. Assuming it still worked, of course.

"If we don't find Nate here, we're going to have to leave the cabin," I told Petra, and explained about the Recall Device.

"Do you know how to get that device working?" she asked.

"Maybe," I said. "It looked like it was working when we were here before, actually. We should take tools from the cabin, though, just in case."

Petra looked skeptical and took Aki outside, carrying her bow with her. I followed as she set the little dromaeosaur down beside the path leading to the dock, the ferns and horsetails providing coverage for him to hide and plenty of bugs to hunt.

Almost immediately, the creature zipped off into the undergrowth.

"Aki!" Petra exclaimed, quickly following, her ankle brace not slowing her down a bit.

"Where is he?" I asked, not seeing him below the shrubbery.

"Over there!" Petra dashed to the edge of the island, where Aki appeared, running through the mud after a dragonfly.

I followed, keeping an eye out for dinosaurs that might not have gotten the message that they shouldn't be able to swim. Also, big giant pterosaurs. Or aquatic reptiles that might launch themselves onto shore, like killer whales after seals.

And that's when the hut with the generator exploded.

NATE

THE GIRL WORE A PITH HELMET OVER SHOULDER-LENGTH BROWN hair and was dressed in long khaki pants and a belted safari jacket. A white blouse and tie showed at her neck. She looked like she might be around sixteen or seventeen years old. By the clothes she was wearing, Nate figured she was from around, maybe, the 1920s or earlier. In one gloved hand, she held a Recall Device. In the other, a revolver.

As the bass boat approached, she raised the gun toward the boys. Silently.

Brady slowed the boat to idle and they came to a stop about five feet away.

"Hello," Brady said, standing and walking to the front as the boat slowly drifted forward.

"Is either of you named Max or Kyle Pierson?" the girl asked.

Nate froze. He didn't recognize the first names, but that was their last name, and since she was holding them at gunpoint, she obviously wasn't a huge friend of the family. "My name's Nate. This is Brady. Who're you?"

"They killed my father," the girl replied.

"They?" Nate asked.

"Max and Kyle Pierson. I believe their sister may have been involved as well."

Brady took in a breath. Nate was dimly aware of his brother stepping forward, which struck him as being a really bad idea if they wanted to get away in a hurry.

"We don't know anyone by those names," Brady told the girl in a soothing tone.

For a moment, she said nothing, and the revolver wavered. "But you are Piersons, yes? You have the look of both Mad Jack and his son, Samuel."

"We don't know a Mad Jack, either," Brady replied carefully. "Or his son."

The girl sneered. "And yet you're here. I believe you did not arrive by autobus."

"What's an autobus?" Nate asked. The girl stared, and Brady gave Nate a look like he thought Nate was an idiot.

"We found one of those round things." Brady nodded at the girl's hand. "In our garage. We seem to have accidentally set it off and it brought us here."

"Where is it now?" she asked.

Brady gestured vaguely behind them. "We lost it in the lake when we arrived."

She was silent, but ever so slightly she shifted the gun toward

Brady. As she was about to speak, there was a rustling in the vegetation about fifty feet behind her. Before any of them could react, three shapes burst from between a pair of cypress trees and lunged forward, splashing through the channel. They were about eight feet tall at the hip, ran on two legs, and had small arms and giant heads with a lot of really sharp teeth.

"Tyrannosaurs!" Brady exclaimed.

The girl whirled and fired the revolver at the dinosaurs and then launched herself toward the boat, crashing into Brady. At the same time, Nate jumped toward the cockpit and landed in the driver's seat. Gritting his teeth against the pain in his leg, he quickly put the throttle into reverse.

The Evinrude outboard roared and shot the boat into the bank of the channel, catching them in a tangle of cypress roots. As Nate struggled to free them, the first of the dinosaurs charged. Brady rolled to the side, and the girl dropped the gun and held up the Recall Device.

Then she threw.

An instant later, there was a pulse of light and a booming sound and Nate felt a wave of air pressure on his face.

When he'd blinked the brightness from his eyes, he saw that the lead dinosaur was gone and the others were fleeing from the sound and light show.

Then he saw, sitting on the edge of the deck just in front of the passenger seat, the girl's revolver. Nate lunged for it just as she spotted it. She kicked out, shoving him to the side. He rolled over and grasped at the boat's deck, knocking the gun into the water. Then his momentum carried him off the edge of the boat.

With a gasp Nate stood, thigh deep in the water, as Brady and the girl got up, both scrambling to find the revolver.

"Leave it," the girl said, standing and straightening her hat. "I used up all the bullets."

"Who are you?" Brady demanded.

"Mildred Campbell is my name," she answered.

The channel wasn't deep, and it was slightly more clear than the lake they'd landed in. It wasn't long before Nate spotted the gun and pulled it up.

Opening the cylinder, he saw she'd been telling the truth. All the chambers were empty. Placing the revolver on the edge of the boat, Nate hoisted himself back aboard.

He limped over to the pilot's seat. "So, Mildred Campbell, who are you?"

"Never mind that!" she replied. "Get us out of here!"

Nate edged the boat forward, intending to go under the fallen tree. "Duck."

"Wait," she said. "Use your Recall Device."

Nate stared. "We don't have a Recall Device."

She looked from Nate to his brother. And then back. "You were telling the truth?"

"Yeah," Nate answered.

Mildred crouched to avoid a hanging branch.

"Why didn't you use your Recall Device to escape instead of throwing it at the tyrannosaur?" Nate asked.

"Because," she answered, "by the time I could have set it to take us anywhere, the tyrannosaur would've been atop us. And the Recall Device has mass limits. You truly do not have a Recall Device? And you're not Max and Kyle?"

Brady and Nate shook their heads.

"Why are you after them?" Brady asked.

As they edged their way under the tree, Mildred explained. "My father used to work with Mad Jack Pierson but became afraid that he was becoming unstable and that leaving a time machine in his hands was dangerous. So my father sought out a person from the future who was important in the development of Mad Jack's Chronal Engine. A girl named Emma. Or Ella." Mildred stood back up and sat in the front fishing chair.

"But what were you doing here?" Nate said.

She sat ramrod straight, regarding the brothers carefully. "I don't know where he obtained his information, but my father's notes indicate that no one used — would be using — the Chronal Engine for nearly a hundred years because the Recall Devices were missing. So I left a Recall Device at the Pierson Ranch barn, where Max and Kyle should've found it. It ought to have brought them here to be trapped and killed in the antediluvian past."

Brady and Nate exchanged a look.

"And now you don't have a way back either?" Brady put in.

Mildred shook her head. "There may be a way. Mad Jack Pierson kept a cabin here for a while. It's only a few miles away on the main body of the lake. Perhaps there's a Recall Device there."

Brady shrugged.

Nate put the throttle up and headed in the direction she pointed.

CHAPTER
VIII

MAX

THE CONCUSSION THREW PETRA AND ME TO THE GROUND. I ROSE shakily to my feet, ignoring the scratches from pebbles in the water where I'd fallen. Ahead of me, Petra adjusted her ankle brace and scooped up a stunned Aki.

"We have to stop the fire before it takes out the cottages," I said. Already, the roof of the dogtrot was igniting from pieces of burning wood that had been thrown onto it from the explosion.

"How?" Petra demanded.

I hesitated. She was right. Buckets would be almost useless, and it wasn't like there was a fire hydrant or even a hose anywhere nearby.

"Then we have to save the stuff in the house," I said. "The tools in the workshop . . . the stuff in the kitchen."

"The cans of food," Petra added.

There was a cracking sound as the wood frame of the generator hut settled in the fire. More sparks flew up, setting the outhouse alight and landing in the weeds next to the dogtrot.

"Come on!" I ran into the passageway and then into the

workshop. Tossing my backpack over one shoulder, I grabbed tools off the pegboard and shoved them into a toolbox, then slammed it shut. Flinging open cabinet doors, I searched for anything that might be useful, then raced outside and put everything down on the dock.

I ran back in as Petra was coming out of the kitchen, a bucket filled with knives and utensils in one hand and a box of cans in another. As the fire grew closer, I grabbed a bunch of pots and the kettle from the stove.

As I made my way out, flames engulfed the roof. Petra dashed into the bedrooms, returning almost immediately with towels and a quilt. We watched, poised at the end of the dock, as the Adirondack chairs in the dogtrot breezeway went up in flames.

"We have to get off the island," Petra said. "The whole thing is going to blow."

"How?" I demanded, gesturing at the pile of supplies we had taken out of the cottages.

"The canoe!" we said at the same time.

We ran around the island, splashing through the shallows. On the other side, the flames had yet to appear. Petra grabbed one end of the canoe and I took the other. We flipped it over; it was heavier than we'd expected. Grabbing the paddles, we dragged the canoe over to the water and launched it just as the flames reached the ginkgo tree next to the cottages.

I'd never actually seen a wood canoe before. Somewhere

between fifteen and twenty feet long, the hull was navy blue and the inside had ribs of a contrasting white wood, lacquered to shine.

I tossed the paddles onto the crossbars and we waded along the shoreline until we reached the pier. Aki climbed into the front seat and then along the side, until he was perched at the bow, like a fluffy figurehead.

We gathered the supplies we'd taken from the dogtrot and carefully arranged them in the canoe so that we didn't puncture a hole in the bottom. Then we hopped aboard — Petra in the back and me in front — and paddled off, toward the closest shore.

Halfway across, we heard a loud crack, so we turned to watch. Black billows of smoke erupted into the sky.

"Well," I said, "it's a pretty good signal fire."

Petra laughed. "Lucky for us."

"Yeah," I muttered, and then said more loudly, "but we're going to have to set up camp somewhere nearby. Maybe put up a real signal fire." That should keep the dinosaurs away. I hoped. "There's a reason Uncle Nate sent us *here*. We need to find him."

"Okay," Petra said, looking over at the shoreline closest to us. "How about over there?" She pointed, and we paddled over.

As I got out and began pulling the canoe up onto the muddy shore, a *Triceratops* appeared at the edge of the forest.

The size of an elephant, the dinosaur was a deep brown in color, with flecks of green. Its frill was a colorful red and orange and blue and had a pattern that looked almost like giant eyes. Of its three horns, the left one had been broken off about halfway down.

Moments later, a second *Triceratops* appeared. And then a third — smaller than the other two— and a fourth. Two more emerged from the forest, both on the small end of the size scale. Which meant that they were part of a mixed-age, possibly family group, which I would have been a lot more thrilled to have learned about if a hundred tons of dinosaur wasn't between us and the nearest dry land.

And then they came toward us.

NATE

As **Nate** continued to steer the bass boat along the shoreline, it began to rain. It was only a brief downpour, and through it all, Mildred sat regally in the forward fishing chair like she owned the thing.

"Should we be doing this?" Brady murmured from where he stood beside his brother. When Nate raised an eyebrow, Brady explained, his voice low. "Taking her to possibly find this Kyle and Max — or maybe even Mad Jack — and, you know, kill them?"

"You think she would?" Nate asked, also whispering.

Brady nodded.

Nate wiped his glasses on his T-shirt. "You have a better idea?"

"Hit her over the head," Brady replied. "Rifle through her pockets, and see if she was telling the truth about being out of bullets. And then shove her overboard."

Nate laughed, then quickly stifled it when Mildred looked back. Obviously, Brady was joking. "No. Let's just keep an eye on her and play it by ear. Besides, we need her to get out of here. Back home, I mean."

"Do we?" Brady asked, softly, then abruptly raised his voice. "I don't like being here."

"In the Cretaceous?" Nate asked. "I thought you *liked* dinosaurs."

"I don't like being in a narrow channel right along the shore where you can't see what could be coming at you," he answered. "Tyrannosaurs aren't the only danger. They just get the most press."

"What else is out there?"

"Dromaeosaurs, troodontids, hadrosaurs, ceratopsians, ankylosaurs, possibly even sauropods. Almost everything you could call a dinosaur. It doesn't have to have big teeth to trample you to death. So we should get out of here as soon as possible."

"When does it get dark?" Nate asked. He didn't know if he wanted to travel without light.

"It'll be a while," Mildred said, swiveling in the fishing chair. "We should make it to the cabin in plenty of time. But if we don't, we can probably tie up for the night somewhere."

Brady shook his head. "We should travel as long as we can. The dinosaurs will be less active after dark."

"No, they won't," Mildred answered.

"What?" Brady said.

"The dinosaur lizards are just as active at night as they are during the day," she replied. "Whoever decided they weren't was just plain wrong."

Brady froze. "Then they're warm-blooded?"

Mildred frowned. "I don't know. It really doesn't get all that cold here at night."

As Brady and Mildred began debating the habits of dinosaurs, Nate tuned them out. He was sticky from sweat and his leg hurt. He was being attacked by mosquitoes and flies. And he was really hungry.

One thought kept cycling through his mind: this was all Dad's fault. That they were still here probably meant he never figured out the Recall Device, and that meant they would be trapped here forever. And why was Dad so obsessed in the first place?

As the channel grew narrower, the number of *Enchodus* swimming past seemed to increase. On both sides, ferns and cycad-like trees vied with cypresses covered in vines.

Every now and then, they came across a fallen branch that they had to move out of the way so the boat could make it through. Once, when Brady was wading through the water, he grabbed a turtle that had been sunning itself on a log in their path and placed it onto the deck of the boat. "Dinner."

It was slow going and they couldn't really see far into the woods. Nate started to wonder how well the girl really knew the area.

After Brady climbed back aboard the boat Nate steered through another logjam and their way began to open up. The channel grew wider and the foliage on either side grew less dense.

Finally, they turned a corner around a stand of cypresses to view a much larger lake. On the far shore, tall evergreens stood in a thick forest. A few islands dotted the smooth water.

And then they saw a greasy billow of smoke arising in the distance from an island on the left.

Mildred frowned. "That's where we're going."

MAX

I PUSHED ON THE CANOE, SLIPPING ONCE IN THE MUD, BUT SOON got the boat floating and moving away from the shore. When the water was a couple of feet deep, I tried to jump aboard, flinging my body across the bow of the canoe. Unfortunately, my momentum carried me over, and the canoe came with me.

As Petra yelled out a warning, the boat capsized, dumping her and all our supplies into the water. Aki landed on my head with a squawk.

Each grabbing an end, together Petra and I righted the canoe, but it was filled with water and too heavy to easily move.

"If we can get it to shore, we can empty it out," Petra said. "When your friend's there" — she pointed at the trike — "go away."

I nodded, though with our luck we'd be just as likely to punch a hole in the bottom of the boat.

Meanwhile, the lead *Triceratops* trundled over to the lake and began drinking. About twenty feet away from us.

Where we were standing the water was about waist deep. As I was wondering if we should stay near the canoe or get out to deeper water away from the trikes, two of the large ones and two of the smaller began rolling in the mud at the edge of the lake.

"Probably keeps the mosquitoes away," Petra said. In one hand she held the bow she had rescued from the lake. She waded over to me and managed to climb inside the canoe to keep everything steady.

As the *Triceratops* finished their mud baths and starting drinking again, we carefully gathered together the supplies that had tipped out the side of the canoe. Most of them were fine, but I supposed the cast-iron utensils would probably rust unless we got them dry. The linens were heavy with water, but at least they sort of floated in the canoe. And as for the Recall Device/Chronal Engine components, who knew what they'd do?

After about an hour, the herd was still behind us but the fire from the island and the dogtrot seemed to have mostly burned down.

"Should we try to get back to the pier?" Petra asked.

By that point, my skin had gotten pruney and I was ready to get out of the water. But the canoe was hard to move and it was still about a hundred yards to the pier, as opposed to ten or so to the shore where the dinosaurs were.

"Let's wait a bit," I said. "The *Triceratops* will probably move on pretty soon."

It actually took another half hour or so. By then, I was slightly disappointed that we hadn't seen anything like a *T. rex* try to hunt

them. On the other hand, I was also kind of glad we hadn't seen anything like a *T. rex* try to hunt them.

"Let's go," Petra said, placing Aki onto the bow of the canoe and clambering out

I glanced toward the island then, and saw, through the smoke beyond, a boat approaching. "Do you see that?"

"A bass boat!" Petra said, and waved wildly.

The boat slowed as it approached the island and began to circle.

"Over here!" I shouted.

"Who are they?" Petra asked.

A girl standing at the front of the boat pointed, and the boat steered toward us. In addition to her, there were two guys in the boat, about my age. The one driving, wearing wire-rimmed glasses, I recognized from family photos as young Uncle Nate. And I also recognized the other, the one wearing a polo shirt. "Oh."

"What is it?" Petra asked.

"Uncle Nate," I said, and swallowed. "And Brady. Uncle Brady."

"I didn't know you had an Uncle Brady," Petra replied.

"I don't," I murmured as the boat came alongside us. "Not anymore."

The girl at the bow was dressed in what looked like a safari outfit you'd see in a Tarzan movie.

"Are you Max Pierson?" the girl asked.

It was actually "Pierson-Takahashi," but she was close enough. Especially since the girl was clearly from the past and the "Takahashi" part might be giving too much away. "Yeah."

In a smooth, swift motion — I almost missed it — she raised a knife from out of nowhere.

"No, don't!" Nate called out just as the girl threw it.

Straight at me.

CHAPTER

XI

NATE

THE BOY — MAX — JUMPED TO THE SIDE WHILE BRADY LAUNCHED himself toward Mildred. Brady got there just after Mildred released the knife, and they both tumbled into the water beside the boat.

Nate stepped forward to see Max get up from beside the swamped canoe and pull the knife from the gunwale. In the meantime, on the other side of the boat, Mildred was shrieking and struggling with Brady, who held on to her, trying to prevent her from getting away.

"Hold it right there!" the girl with Max shouted. "Don't move!" She held a compound bow with an arrow nocked and aimed at Mildred, string pulled back and ready to release.

Brady backed away from Mildred, and Max stepped to the other girl's side, dripping, holding the knife in one hand.

"Who are you?" Max demanded.

"I'm Nate Pierson. That's my brother, Brady, and the girl who threw the knife is Mildred Campbell."

Until then, Nate hadn't been sure if Mildred had been telling

the truth about her past. But from the look on Max's face, it seemed she was. Or at least some of it. "You recognize the name?"

"A man named Isambard Campbell kidnapped my sister and tried to kill me," Max answered. "And he was also out to get Mad Jack Pierson."

"Lies!" Mildred screamed. "You killed my father! My father *helped* Mad Jack build the Chronal Engine but came to realize Mad Jack would never use it wisely!"

"This is our friend Petra Castillo." Max gestured toward the girl with the bow. "She, my brother, Kyle, and I came back here to save my sister, Emma, from Campbell."

"And the three of you killed him!" Mildred said.

Max shook his head. "Petra and Kyle were back at our camp. Samuel and I were trying to rescue Emma when Campbell came after us, shooting. He stumbled onto a nesting *T. rex* and . . . got eaten." Max grimaced. "He tried to use a Recall Device to get away, but the mass overloaded the machine and . . ." Max raised his hands. "I don't know what happened afterward."

"He materialized in our backyard, burned and in severe pain," Mildred said, her voice icy. "But he did say before he died that you were responsible."

Max winced. "I'm sorry he died. But he was trying to kill us."

As Mildred bristled again, Petra gestured with the bow. "Stay."

"Did you say 'Samuel'?" Brady put in, which seemed to Nate to be the least important part of the story.

"My great-grandfather," Max said. "Although he was young at the time."

"Our grandfather is named Samuel," Nate said, staring at Max. "Does that mean you're . . ."

"Yes. You're my uncle—*uncles*," Max answered. "Your sister, Ernestine, is my mother."

As Nate tried to absorb the fact that Ernie had, or would have, three kids, Max spoke again. "You, Brady. Make sure she doesn't have any more knives."

"You're not touching me!" Mildred said, stepping back.

"Petra could just shoot you," Brady told her.

Silently, Mildred unbuttoned her jacket and allowed Brady to check if she had any more weapons. "She's clean."

Petra lowered the bow and returned the arrow to the quiver on her back.

"Do you have a Recall Device?" Nate asked Max. "Can you get us home?"

"Well," Max said, "about that . . ."

MAX

"It was stolen," I said, and looked at Mildred. "Maybe *she* had something to do with that."

I'd never thought of Isambard Campbell as having a family. He was just the former assistant or graduate student or whatever who had kidnapped Emma and tried to kill us last time we were here. Yesterday, in fact. As for our Recall Device, it made sense that Mildred had taken it to trap us here. But she didn't admit or deny anything.

"Stolen?" Brady repeated as he took another step back from her. "So you don't actually have a way back home?"

I hesitated. "Not exactly. But I have an idea. There's a chance that there's a steamboat on the shore of the seaway not far from here that may have a functioning Recall Device. But I don't know what kind of condition it's in. I think the boat originally belonged to Great-Great-Grandpa Pierson, but it has a big hole in the side." I shrugged. "I don't know how it ended up there."

"How far is that?" Nate asked.

"A couple days maximum, I think," I told them. I'd never

made the trip by boat, but it seemed as though it would be faster than walking. I gestured at the canoe. "Brady, can you give us a hand here?"

As Brady came over, Petra stepped beside me, and I whispered to her, "Keep an eye on Mildred."

Petra nodded and reached out to pet Aki, who'd been sitting on the bow of the canoe.

"What is that?" Mildred asked, staring at the chick.

"A dromaeosaur hatchling," Petra said.

"That's a dromaeosaur?" Brady exclaimed, leaning closer. He glanced at me. "Covered in down? Does that mean they have feathers as adults?"

I hesitated over how much I should tell him. I decided that this, at least, really wouldn't matter. "Yes, although fossil feathers on dinosaurs aren't going to be found until the 1990s."

"Are there woolly tyrannosaurs too?" he asked. "Or just dromaeosaurs?"

"Guys," Petra said, "could you do the whole *Walking with Dinosaurs* thing later?"

With that, the three of us hauled the canoe toward shore. Nate steered the bass boat up behind, and Mildred waded through the water a bit off to the side, giving me looks that would've killed me if she'd been able to shoot lasers out of her eyes.

Once we got the canoe to shore, Petra held out her hand for Aki, who immediately jumped on it.

Nate dropped anchor but stayed aboard the bass boat and didn't get out to help.

"He got bit," Brady said, at my glance. "By a mosasaur."

"You've been at sea?" I asked.

Brady shook his head, pointing back the way they'd come. "Up that way. In the lake. A *freshwater* mosasaur."

"Here?" I said. "Really?"

"They haven't discovered freshwater mosasaurs in your time?" Brady asked with a grin.

"Not in North America," I told him.

"Guys . . ." Petra said again.

"Unc — Nate — if you see something moving in the forest, yell," I called out.

"What left these tracks?" Brady asked.

"*Triceratops,*" I told him. "A mixed adult-juvenile group." I pointed out where they had come through from the forest to take their mud bath.

Brady's eyes widened, but he didn't say anything.

We unloaded the canoe while Mildred came over and peered closely at Aki. I couldn't hear what she and Petra were saying, but the Campbell girl seemed transfixed by the dromaeosaur. Which was fine with me.

Once it was clear of supplies, Brady and I tipped the canoe over, emptying out the water.

"How big will it get?" Brady asked. "The dromaeosaur?"

"About four feet long, three feet high at the waist," I told him. That, at least, was its mother's size.

As we reloaded the canoe, Petra and Mildred stepped close. Aki, I noticed, was now perched on Mildred's shoulder.

"It's getting late," Petra said. "We need to find shelter and get dry."

"Back to the island?" I suggested.

Petra scrunched her nose. "It'll be a little charred."

"We could sleep on the boat." I used my hand to shield my eyes from the sun. "It looks like the dock is still there, mostly. And it's probably safer there than here." That was why Mad Jack had built the cabin, after all.

It ended up being a weird night. Most of the dogtrot had burned, but we managed to salvage some bits for firewood. We discovered that the backpack was waterproof, so Petra put on my extra set of clothes — T-shirt and cargo shorts. Mildred wore Petra's spares, although she had to be reassured that they were actually girls' clothes. She seemed to feel they were inappropriate, or at least inappropriate to wear in the company of human males.

We ate an *Enchodus* that Nate had caught earlier, cooked whole, and broke into one of the cans of peas and another of baked beans. The fish wasn't great, but at least it was filling.

We decided to keep watch, in part because we didn't know

who had stolen the Recall Device, in part because of the risk of dinosaurs, and in part because Mildred wanted to kill me.

Mildred and Petra stretched a quilt on a rope to make a wall and provide a "separate bedchamber," and they built their own fire so they could dry their clothes.

For the first watch, I sat up with Petra. I wasn't sure I felt all that safe with Mildred on the island and a machete in arm's reach. But at least we wouldn't let her take a watch by herself.

For a while, Petra and I were silent, just looking into the fire and listening to the screeches and animal calls from the forest across the water. Then my thoughts drifted toward Campbell and Mildred. She'd said her father hadn't really been trying to kill us. I wasn't sure I believed that, though. He'd kidnapped Emma and then came after us with a gun, through a tyrannosaur-infested forest. And he'd never once said anything to Emma about saving the time stream. She definitely would've mentioned it if he had.

As for Mildred trying to kill me, that was more than a little scary. It was bad enough that there were giant reptilian predators out here.

"So what's the story with Brady?" Petra asked, startling me.

It took me a moment to arrange my thoughts. "It's kind of creeping me out." I hesitated, watching the light from the fire flicker across her face. "Grandpa never mentioned him?" Petra had lived on the ranch with her mother for the past several years, and Grandpa never left the place. I sort of figured he might've said something or that it might've come up somehow.

"No. Honestly, though, he only rarely mentioned Nate, or your mom, either." For a moment we watched as Aki tussled with fish guts before devouring the *Enchodus*'s liver.

"He's Nate's twin," I said, lowering my voice and double-checking to make sure the other three were asleep. "Fraternal, obviously. He was a volunteer fireman. He died when I was about a year old, so I don't have any memories of him."

"How did he die?"

I plucked at a fern frond and tore it apart. "He was at the Ismay High School football stadium fire when the concourse collapsed."

Petra gasped.

"Yeah." I shook my head. "He led a group of kids from St. Alphonsus Elementary School out from the upper deck and down the stairs and was going back up to get some more folks out of one of the skyboxes when the whole side of the stadium fell over."

Until now, it had only really been a story.

"I'm sorry," Petra said.

"Thanks," I replied. I let out a breath. "I didn't actually know him, though. Until now, he's always been just a name and a bunch of photos."

Petra stared across the fire, to where Brady and Nate were asleep. "But why is it creeping you out?"

I glanced over, watching the shadows from the flames play over her profile. "Because in our time, Brady's dead!"

Petra gave the fish carcass a little nudge with a stick. Aki pounced. "But in our time, so's Mildred. Probably. And so was your Great-Grandfather Samuel, too."

"I know," I answered. "But they're supposed to be! Brady's . . . Brady is Nate's age and should be living his life now. Then. Whatever."

"Are you thinking of telling him?"

"Yes. Maybe. I don't know."

"Would you want to know?" Petra asked.

I took a deep breath. "Yes. Maybe. I don't know. And if I do tell him, what if that changes everything? What if he never saves those kids?"

"What if your telling him *is* what saves those kids?"

< 78 >

NATE

To Nate, the night felt odd.

He wasn't sure what to make of any of the three strangers. Mildred he could sort of understand, although her wanting vengeance for the death of her father seemed either a bit old-fashioned or a bit insane. Nate couldn't imagine going to these lengths to avenge his own father's death, although part of that might have been because his leg throbbed through the night, even though he'd taken most of the aspirin.

He could definitely see Brady doing it, though.

They had made sure to keep Mildred away from Petra's bow and arrows and anything else that was pointy or sharp.

"She might decide to throw rocks or stuff at you, though," Brady had told Max. "Or push you in the lake. You can swim, right?"

Max didn't look amused.

Petra seemed solid enough and had survival skills that could be useful. And the baby dromaeosaur thing was either adorable or deeply disturbing. From what Brady said, the creatures could grow bigger than turkey vultures and were a lot deadlier.

Then there was Max himself, who seemed kind of like a know-it-all and a little freaked out around Brady. Nate didn't think his brother realized that, though, possibly because he and Max were bonding over the whole dinosaur thing. Also, Max was Nate and Brady's nephew and Ernie's son and Nate didn't really need to know that. Maybe time travel was a bad idea after all.

And this plan of Max's seemed completely insane. The chances that they could salvage something that worked from a wrecked boat seemed really, really remote. And he wasn't convinced Max had a real idea of how the thing worked. Forget ending up in a particularly bad time of history when they didn't have plumbing or antibiotics. They could materialize inside a wall.

And, yes, Nate was slightly feverish and it was hot out.

The air was thick, although not quite as bad as it was during the day. Loud insects seemed to surround them. Occasionally, there were calls from deep in the forest across the lake, like nothing Nate had ever heard before. Hooting and screeching, sure, but from no animal he could identify.

Later, toward the middle of the night, he and Brady sat talking on the charred surface of the dock, legs dangling just above the water.

"What do you think?" Brady asked. He'd nudged Nate awake when it was time for their watch. The others were snoring softly.

"We can never tell Ernie about this," Nate replied, gesturing to where Max was sleeping.

Brady nodded. "She'll probably like him, though. She'll have to if she's his mother."

"You don't?"

"He seems a little . . . edgy around me."

"Yeah," Nate answered. "I noticed that too."

At dawn, Nate was awakened by the screaming of birds and who knows what else. Brady said that songbirds hadn't evolved yet, and Max added that it was probably the theropod dinosaurs, the pterosaurs, and possibly something called *Icthyornis*.

The girls still seemed asleep on their side of the camp.

Nate's leg felt tender to the touch and the skin was tight and warm. The bites still seemed to be oozing. They were clearly infected, but there wasn't a lot he could do about it right then.

He was determined not to complain but groaned when he realized there was no more aspirin.

"Here," Max said, his voice low when he realized what Nate was upset about. He pulled a red pouch from his backpack and tossed it toward Nate. "There should be some painkillers in there."

When Nate opened the first-aid pouch, a small object fell out, about the size and shape of a package of PEZ. He swallowed a couple aspirins before picking it up. The end pulled off like a pen cap to reveal a metal connector of some kind. Written in black marker on the side was the word NICE.

"What is this?" he asked, holding it up.

"It's called a USB flash drive," Max answered, eyebrows raised. "I didn't pack it, though."

"Then who did?" Brady put in.

"My brother . . . or uncle." Max reached to take the gadget and the pouch from Nate.

"A drive?" Nate asked, still not really understanding. "You mean, like a floppy disk drive?"

"Yeah, but with a lot bigger capacity." Max tossed it up and caught it in his hand a couple of times, frowning in concentration.

"How much bigger?"

"At least a gigabyte," Max answered, still frowning.

"What?" Nate exclaimed. "On that?" That was like a super-computer level of memory.

"Uh-huh."

"So did you bring a computer?" Brady put in.

"No," Max replied. "That's what's weird. I brought one last time, but I don't have it now . . . He did say, 'Play nice,' though. Which means it must be important."

"Who?" Nate asked.

"You," Max replied.

"So why would Kyle or your Uncle Nate send this with you if you don't have anything to play it on?" Brady asked.

"Maybe they'll send something," Petra said as she emerged from behind the quilt.

"You heard?" Max asked.

"It's a blanket," she answered, "not a brick wall."

"Fascinating as this is, if we can't do anything with that . . . whatever it is, perhaps we should get moving," Mildred put in.

At that, Max zipped the drive back into the first-aid pouch and returned it to his backpack.

They decided to leave the canoe at the island because towing it with the bass boat would have been too complicated. Brady and Max hauled it out of the water and placed it upside down on logs next to the charred remains of the cabin itself. The two did one last search around the island while Petra and Mildred hunted Aki. That is, they watched while Aki hunted in the mud for crabs and worms and such.

In the embers of the fire, they cooked the turtle Brady had caught, then pried off its shell and had it for breakfast with a can of creamed corn and another of red beans. After that, they were off. Nate took the driver's seat and Mildred went up front to the fishing chair, back in her safari garb and pith helmet. Petra sat cross-legged beside her, while Brady took the rear fishing seat and Max sat next to Nate.

Ahead of them, a trio of big *Quetzalcoatlus* landed and began wading through the water like giant storks.

The boat still had three-quarters of a tank of gas. Nate wasn't sure how far they were going, so he kept the boat at a relatively sedate pace. Not so slow as to not leave a wake, but not exactly winning any speed records.

He took them away from the island and toward the river. It wasn't all that wide — it kind of reminded Nate of the Colorado River as it ran through Bastrop. Maybe about a hundred yards across, but more winding.

As they entered the mouth of the river, the pterosaurs took off, alarmed by the sound of the motor. To Nate, they really were amazing. He would've enjoyed watching them more if he had been certain of a way back home and if his leg wasn't still hurting.

It hadn't really cooled off during the night and was already getting steamier.

MAX

I WATCHED AS THE *QUETZALCOATLUS* TOOK OFF AND THEN CIRCLED around and flew inland. There was just something absolutely incredible about a creature that big that could fly.

To our right, on the far side of the river, a flock of wading birds, like herons, strutted amid a growth of horsetails. I kept an eye out on the left for *Triceratops*.

Behind me, now in the fishing seat, Brady craned his neck, trying to take in everything. Nate didn't seem to be all that inter-ested in where we were, but his leg looked really ugly — purple and swollen — and had to be hurting. We needed to make it home soon. The infection could kill him just as easily as a tyrannosaur.

I hadn't actually slept all that well last night, a combination of damp clothes and the fact that I didn't want Mildred to lop off my head with a machete or anything. This morning, as we made breakfast, she kept giving me the evil eye.

"So," Brady asked, "anyone ever try to kill you before?"

I stared. "What do you think?"

He shrugged. "For all I know, y'all are living in some hellishly radioactive, postapocalyptic place where gasoline is the most valuable commodity in the world."

"Yes," I told him. "That's exactly what the future is like." I was tempted to say that we were also fighting a battle against a race of sentient machines, but decided that even letting him know what the future *wasn't* wasn't a good idea. Although there was a lot he was already picking up. Like the fact that his sister would have three kids.

"Have the Cubs won a World Series lately?" Brady asked next.

I tried to figure out if he was serious. "You're a Cubs fan?"

"No," Nate put in, "but Ernie's idiot boyfriend, Jacob Takahashi, is." He shrugged. "He's from Chicago."

I tried not to change my expression at Nate's mentioning my father. Or the fact that Nate didn't like him.

But Nate saw me react. "You know the name."

"I can't tell you," I said.

"About the Cubs, or Jacob Takahashi?" Brady said.

"Either."

CHAPTER
XV

NATE

THE RIVER WAS FLOWING FAST ENOUGH THAT NATE DIDN'T REALLY have to keep the throttle all that high. Just enough so they had power to steer around rocks.

Max had moved to sit on the deck in front of the cockpit, while Brady was in a seat next to his brother. Petra and Mildred were still up front, playing with Aki and keeping a lookout for whatever was ahead.

On the left, the riverbank varied between three and ten feet high, concave with exposed sand and rock and tree roots. Above was a forest of redwoods and ferns. On the right, the riverbank was lower and the trees weren't as big. Most resembled modern oaks and magnolias, though there were still some redwoods. On each side, ferns and palmettos and cycads formed the undergrowth.

As the boat came around a bend in the river, ahead of them, on the high bank to the left, stood a huge row of dinosaurs, about a hundred yards long, pawing at the ground, looking like they were trying to decide if they wanted to jump in. From the noise – sort of like mooing, but with loud screeches mixed in — it seemed to be a huge herd. They were four-legged, dark brown with green stripes and lighter underbellies. Nate guessed they ranged from around twenty to thirty feet long. Their heads looked sort of like those of horses, but with wide, flat mouths.

"That's incredible!" Max murmured. "Proof of migratory behavior — "

"Here be dragons," Brady said.

"What?" Nate asked.

But before Brady answered, Max did. "Supposedly ancient map makers would inscribe 'Here be dragons' on areas they didn't actually know about."

Brady gave Max an indulgent glance but didn't otherwise respond.

These were pretty tame-looking dragons, Nate thought. Granted, they were impressively large, but they didn't have great big fangs or incisors or anything, and they didn't breathe fire.

"Umm," he said, just to be sure, "these dinosaurs don't breathe fire, do they?"

"Of course not," Brady said, his attention back on the herd gathered on the riverbank.

Max cleared his throat. "Well — "

"They breathe fire?" Brady exclaimed, now staring at their nephew.

Max squirmed. "Technically, we don't actually know. Because, you know, we only have bones for the most part, and soft tissue in a few cases, but not all the organs and – "

"I want a dragon," Petra said, while Mildred snorted in a not altogether ladylike fashion.

"You *have* a dragon," Brady pointed out.

"So, what are they?" Nate asked.

"Hadrosaurs of some kind," Brady said. "They're sort of the cows of the Cretaceous."

"Probably *Kritosaurus*," Max said.

Nate stared at the gathered herd and adjusted the throttle to hold position. "If they want to cross the river, what are they waiting for?"

"Those!" Petra said, pointing at a series of huge shapes low in the river. "And over there!"

In the water, farther down on a sandbar in the middle of the river, were alligators, but bigger than any Nate had ever seen. Or heard of. Maybe forty feet long, they were at least twice the length of the bass boat.

"*Deinosuchus!*" Brady and Max said at the same time.

At that moment, the first of the hadrosaurs jumped into the water.

"Nate, get us out of here!" Max shouted, just as the boat lurched from a blow underneath and Nate was thrown back into his seat in the cockpit.

Nate glanced over the side and saw a huge scaly green shape shoot out from under the boat, thumping the aluminum hull as it scraped by.

Finally, when the creature's head was much farther away than it properly should've been, the boat settled.

On his knees at the bow, Brady yelled, "Nate! We need warp speed now or we're all dead!"

If Nate punched it, it would be like running into a wall. He glanced behind. That was blocked too. "There are too many of them!"

By then, the wall of hadrosaurs on shore had broken as one after another jumped into the river, a steady stream of dinosaurs. Nate tried to keep the boat steady, looking out for a clear path, even as the gators attacked the *Kritosaurus*. One of the giant reptiles would latch on to a leg and pull the entire hadrosaur under, twisting in a frenzy of white water, tearing off chunks of flesh.

Even as Nate maneuvered the boat around one and then another, in no time they were surrounded by a steady flow of hadrosaurs, *Deinosuchus* in their midst, picking them off one after another. The bass boat bobbed as the gators jostled it from underneath and the *Kritosaurus* struck its sides.

"This may take a while to get through." Max crouched at the front of the boat, right behind the trolling motor, glancing from one side of the river to the other. Petra stood, leaning against the fishing seat, holding on with one hand, the other holding the bow, an arrow nocked loosely. Only a handful of the first hadrosaurs had made it across. The rest of the herd was pouring into the water, though.

As the boat held steady in the middle of the river, another gator approached. It knocked into the side of the boat, then passed by, so the group got a close-up of the armor on its back along the entire length of the hull. Then it dived after a carcass.

As the boat was being battered about, Petra knelt, one hand on the fishing seat. The others hung on as best they could. It was like being on a particularly scary thrill ride, only it wasn't a ride.

"We have to get out of here!" Petra said.

Nate sat behind the wheel, hand on the throttle. "Give me a heading!"

"Left!" Max shouted as they headed directly toward a pair of giant gators.

"That's 'port,'" Brady corrected.

"Now straight," Max yelled. Nate steered the boat between a pair of hadrosaurs, passing directly in front of a third. The giant herbivore ignored them and just kept swimming straight ahead. A moment later, they were out of its path and had dodged another gator.

Within minutes, though, they bobbed from the impact of another *Deinosuchus*. Then a *Kritosaurus* rammed the side of the boat, deflecting it from its course and into the path of another dino. For a moment, the front of the boat tilted downward as the creature rested its four-foot-long head on the bow, crushing the trolling motor. The bass boat slowed and turned, the giant herbivore dragging it along.

"Get it off!" Nate yelled, and tried to reverse to pull free. But with gators and hadrosaurs all around, there wasn't any room to maneuver.

"How?" Max yelled. Sitting, he braced himself and kicked out at the *Kritosaurus*'s head.

Water sloshed over the front of the boat as the weight of the creature bore it down.

"Use the machete—" Mildred began.

Then the hadrosaur's flank was struck by a gator. Instantly, the boat bobbed back up and surged backwards.

"Other way!" Brady shouted. The path ahead was now clear.

Nate punched it.

That's when there was a surge from underneath, and the back of the boat rose, the propeller grinding in open air. Before Nate could react, the bass boat tipped over onto its port side.

When it righted itself, water cascading off the deck, Petra was clinging to the support of the front fishing chair and Brady was braced in the seat behind Nate.

Max and Mildred were gone.

MAX

I SURFACED, BLINKING WATER OUT OF MY EYES, AND THRASHED MY head from side to side to get my bearings. For the moment, I was surrounded by hadrosaurs and carcasses. There didn't seem to be any of the giant alligators close by. I spotted my backpack about ten feet away, bobbing with the current. In a few strokes, I reached it, looping one strap over my arm. Then I treaded water, trying to avoid being swum over by the herbivores. The current was stronger than I'd expected, propelling me downriver next to the bloody carcass of a *Kritosaurus*. To my left, beyond the body, I could see the boat. I raised my hand, waving and yelling, and then realized that I needed to get out of the river and away from the dead hadrosaur as fast as I could before another *Deinosuchus* appeared.

I grabbed at the neck ridge of a swimming *Kritosaurus*, letting it pull me toward the riverbank, about twenty yards away.

The creature touched bottom before I did. As it surged to its feet, I rolled away, put my head down, and swam hard. Finally, when

I could touch bottom, I high-stepped toward the bank and hauled myself onto dry land. As I glanced back, I saw the *Kritosaurus's* body bob as it was grabbed from underneath by a *Deinosuchus*.

I spotted a few of the *Kritosaurus* climbing out onto the bank upriver, shaking off the water, and then re-forming the herd. Steadying myself by grabbing on to a cypress branch, I turned and saw the bass boat about a hundred yards ahead, heading downriver. Sideways.

"Nate!" I yelled. "Petra! Brady!"

Silence. Except for the thrashing of predators and the cries and grunts of the kritosaurs.

"Mildred!" I called, just because.

Then I ran along the riverbank to try to catch up to the boat.

As I dodged a cycad, I tripped over something lying in my path. I went sprawling, half into the river, the wind knocked out of me. Praying that it wasn't a *Deinosuchus*, I rolled over and saw it was Mildred.

She coughed, then sat up, her hand on her side where I'd kicked her when I fell. Her hat was missing and her khaki safari outfit was now soaked and streaked with mud.

I stepped back, holding my hands up, ready for her to shove me back into the alligator-infested water. "Don't."

She stood, without any help from me. "I'm not going to. I need you to get me out of here."

I hesitated, not sure if I could trust her. On the other hand, I wasn't going to push her into the river. I was just going to have to be careful. And make sure I kept her in sight at all times.

"Come on," I said. "If we hurry, we can catch up to the boat."

Mildred stared. "The boat has a motor, does it not? Surely they'll just come back for us?"

"If they can," I replied, beginning to walk. "But they're going to need to know where we are to come back to, don't you think?"

Behind us, in the water, a pair of *Deinosuchus* fought over the carcass of one of the hadrosaurs. Farther upriver, the last of the herd seemed to have entered the water. At different spots along the bank, dead hadrosaurs floated, some being pulled apart by the gators.

We followed the curve of the river as the boat floated ahead of us. Then it disappeared from view.

We continued on for about half an hour after we lost sight of the bass boat, dodging trees and ferns, following the riverbank. As we poked through a thick stand of cycads, Mildred stopped abruptly.

Ahead of us, drinking water from a creek that ran into the river, was a *T. rex.*

NATE

"WHERE ARE THEY?" PETRA SHOUTED.

The boat continued sideways, still perched on the giant gator's back, the propeller on the motor spinning uselessly in the air. They were surrounded by gators and hadrosaur bodies, and Nate couldn't see Max or Mildred anywhere.

Finally, they came to a drifting carcass and the *Deinosuchus* dived, pulling the dead hadrosaur under.

The propeller caught the water again and the boat surged forward. Nate cut the wheel to the right to avoid another of the gators and headed back upriver to find Max and Mildred.

As the boat turned, it was struck again from the rear. The outboard motor screeched, and they lurched to a stop.

"Turn it off!" Brady yelled. "Let me see."

Nate killed the ignition and hit the control to lift the motor.

"Where are they?" Petra asked again, peering upriver and steadying herself with a hand on the windshield.

"I don't know," Brady said. "But the propeller's bent."

Which meant the motor was useless. They weren't going to be able to get the missing two.

"Bend it back!" Petra snapped.

"You got a wrench?" Brady asked. "Or a sledgehammer?"

Nate lowered the motor back into the water so they could at least steer. But they didn't have any forward control. They were stuck with where the river was taking them.

"Are they still in the water?" Brady asked, staring back over the corpse-littered river.

"I don't see them," Petra said, gnawing her lip.

"If they are . . ." Nate began.

"They can swim," Petra interrupted. "At least Max can. I think. His sister's on the swim team . . ."

As her voice trailed off, Nate did not point out that that didn't really mean anything. And that Max could've hit his head on a rock. "They'll try to make it ashore."

"Which side?" Petra asked.

"I don't know," Nate replied. "I don't even know if we're ahead of them."

"Doesn't matter," Brady said. "Nate, take us to the shore and we'll wait a bit. If they made it out of the water, they'll see us, whatever side of the river they're on."

"Unless they've already passed us," Nate told him.

"In that case, we'll just push off again and catch up," Petra said.

"Even without the motor, we'll still be faster than they would be on foot."

"What if they're still in the water?" Nate asked.

Brady gestured as a *Deinosuchus* swam by. "Then they won't be for long."

MAX

I'VE ALWAYS LIKED *TYRANNOSAURUS REX*. THEY'RE AWESOME, WITH six-foot skulls and ridiculously tiny arms and teeth the size of hunting knives. They've got a great one at the Field Museum in Chicago. It's my favorite. It's big. It's dead.

This one wasn't.

The forty-foot-long theropod was looking away from us, at a slight angle, head down as it scooped water into its mouth.

"Back. Away. Very. Very. Slowly." I glanced behind us, to make sure of my route. We retreated, keeping a close eye on the huge animal.

Then, for some reason, the *T. rex* swung its giant head toward the water. I was puzzled at first, but then I saw the head of a *Deinosuchus* slowly swimming downriver. Toward the *T. rex*.

I'd seen too many pictures and articles speculating on just this: the two biggest predators of the time going head to head. The alligator and the dinosaur were oblivious to us. For a moment, I paused.

"Are you addled?" Mildred said in a loud whisper. "We have to get past that thing! Now's our chance!"

I suppressed a sigh and we continued edging away, then turned and walked into the woods, away from the river and away from the *T. rex*. We stayed under the cover of the trees, hoping that we'd be safer there than in open ground.

After about fifteen minutes, we climbed up an embankment next to a waterfall and crossed the creek.

"We have to return to the river," Mildred said.

I nodded, resisting the temptation to tell her she was only stating the obvious. I was more concerned that we had no way of knowing if Petra and my uncles had stopped upriver or whether we were farther along than they were. At least we all knew where we were heading—to Mad Jack's steamboat with the Recall Device, which hopefully still worked.

If they were smart, though, they would head downriver a ways and then wait for us, knowing that they were a lot faster on the water than we were on land.

And we needed to find them. I had the backpack Kyle had given me, with a hunting knife and a canteen and the fire-starting kit, but that was about it for our supplies.

Also, there was the fact that I was traveling with a girl who would be just as happy to see me dead and might even be willing to clock me over the head with a rock.

"I'm not going to kill you now," Mildred interrupted my thoughts, seemingly reading them, as we trudged along toward the river.

"What?"

"As I told you before, I'm not going to kill you now," she said. "Insofar as you're the only one who can get us out of here and back home, so you're safe until then."

"You're not making me feel any better," I told her, because she was obviously thinking about it. On the other hand, if she was telling the truth, I wouldn't have to watch out for tyrannosaurs and psychopaths at the same time.

Before long, the ground grew wetter and muddier. Soon, our shoes were sinking into the muck, and our progress slowed. The low-lying marshy area was teeming with life, but not the cute cuddly kind. Mosquitoes and dragonflies buzzed around my face and the water. Even more insects scrambled on the surface tension of slow-moving stagnant areas. I walked into a spider web strung across a pair of fern trees in front of me.

Overhead, something chittered in the trees. I looked up but didn't see anything other than a lizard clinging to a cypress trunk.

My stomach grumbled and my back felt damp with sweat. We continued on, and I said a prayer of thanks that I'd grown up in an era with air conditioning.

As I glanced underneath a cycad frond, something caught my eye. Concealed with a camouflage of brown markings was a tiny little dinosaur. A hypsilophodont of some kind, I figured. Small, about four feet long, relatively harmless. The deer of the Cretaceous.

I knelt and looked closer. It stared at me with unblinking eyes. It looked almost like a hawk, but with no feathers and a beak-like snout filled with teeth. I grabbed a stick and thrust it at the creature. It jumped up and sped past me before I could react. It had been sitting on a nest, all right, just as I had figured, but there were no eggs.

I got off my knees and took another look around. The clicking and chirping of insects and birds were the only sounds. The air was still and full of moisture. I peered into the narrow channel separating us from another piece of land. Underneath a fallen branch, I could make out a shape moving against the weak current. An alligator, about two feet long.

I crouched low, trying to make as little noise as possible, while the alligator swam past. Then I jumped in the water, hands in front of me, and reached to snatch it. I couldn't quite get hold of it with my hands, but my momentum trapped it against a patch of ferns. The animal thrashed a couple times and bit me on the arm once before I was able to get it under control – that is, stun it – and slip it into my backpack.

"Dinner," I told Mildred.

"Poetic justice," she replied.

"Yeah," I replied. "I was thinking the same thing."

At least we wouldn't go hungry, although I had no idea how to cook the reptile. I looked at the blood running down my arm. After uncorking my canteen, I poured a little water onto the wound to clean it out. I decided then I didn't like swamps. And my fingers and probably my toes were pruney.

Not long after that, we finally made it back to the main body of the river.

We stood at a curve with a good view in both directions. A *Kritosaurus* carcass floated past, but there was no sign of the bass boat.

"Climb a tree, maybe?" Mildred said.

I went up a cypress that stood at the edge of the river. But I saw nothing.

CHAPTER
XIX

NATE

THE BOAT RESTED AT ANCHOR ALONG THE RIVERBANK, TIED UP NEXT to a small island formed by a pair of cypresses growing from the water. Branches and other detritus had built up and collected enough sand and dirt for ferns and small shrubs to have grown up around them.

Every now and then, a bloody limb from one of the hadrosaurs drifted by. Smaller alligators would grab the limbs and pull their meal under.

On the bank, about three feet above where they'd anchored the boat, Petra stood and watched, holding on to her bow with one hand, arrow loosely nocked. "Just in case," she said. Aki lay beside her on a rock, drying his feathers in the hot sun.

Nate wasn't sure whether Petra was watching the water for a chance to rescue the others, or looking for their bodies. At that point, he didn't think it was likely that they'd see them alive. The gators seemed to be pretty thorough. On the other hand, there were a lot of the *Kritosaurus* parts floating downriver, so it was possible that Max and Mildred had escaped just by virtue of numbers. There were a lot of other things to eat besides them.

When Nate mentioned this to his brother, Brady just murmured, "Yes. That's the whole point of herds."

Nate's leg felt warm and clammy, and throbbed when he moved it. And he still felt too warm.

While they waited, Brady peered over the side of the boat, into the ferns and undergrowth.

"What are you looking at?" Nate asked.

His brother jumped overboard and landed in ankle-deep water, then bent over and pulled up a length of hadrosaur leg. It was about three feet long, including the hoof.

"Beef for dinner!" he said, handing it to Nate. Then he grabbed Nate's hand to pull himself back aboard.

Nate sniffed it. "Will it keep?"

Brady looked at him like he was an idiot, then pointed to the live well at the rear of the boat. "This is insulated like a thermos."

Nate didn't point out their lack of ice, but placed the leg into the well as Brady took off his shoes and socks to dry. "Do you really think we're going to find them?" Nate asked.

Brady hesitated. "I think so. I mean, Max came here to find us, right? He wants to find us as much as we want to find him. Plus there's Petra. And he knows the only way back. So eventually we're going to find each other again. Maybe not until we reach the sea." At his last words, he glanced up at Petra on the riverbank.

"Unless there's another way back," Nate said. "In which case, he might be superfluous to the time stream."

"Don't tell Petra that," Brady warned.

After that, the brothers were quiet, occasionally splashing water on their faces to cool down. In the distance, they heard the chirping of insects and calls of birds and who knew what else.

While they waited, Brady grabbed the machete and climbed up the riverbank. Nate didn't hear what he said to Petra, but together they disappeared for a moment. When they returned, each was carrying a ten-foot pole. Nate did not make the obvious joke.

"We don't have any oars or paddles, so I thought we could use these," Brady said, laying them down along the sides of the boat.

Finally, after another hour or so had elapsed, Petra jumped back down into the boat. "It'll be dark soon. Let's find a place where we can build a bonfire."

They used the poles to push off from the island and got underway, traveling with the current. Nate steered the boat as best he could, trying to keep close to the riverbank.

They let the river carry them for a while, spotting birds along the bank, an occasional feathered thing wading in the shallows. Every now and then, a creek opened into the river.

As the shadows got longer, Nate steered the boat around a bend, the sun reflecting off a large object wedged between a tree and the riverbank. An object that was green and shiny and metallic and had no business being in the Cretaceous. It looked a little strange and appeared to be lying on its side, but Nate could've sworn it was a VW Beetle.

"What is that?" Brady asked, standing.

"It's a VW Beetle," Petra said. "We brought it last time we were here."

Nate steered the boat closer. "Is it, like, a concept-car version of a VW Beetle?" It looked to be the same shape as a standard Beetle to Nate, but it seemed bigger, smoother, more aerodynamic. And less solid, somehow.

Petra shook her head. "No, it's a regular production model. A nice one too, with a Bose sound system and —" Her eyes widened. "We have to find Max!"

"Yeah . . ." Brady said, as he and Nate exchanged a look.

"No — I mean, the car has an accessory port for plugging a USB drive into! *That's* why the drive was in the first-aid kit! There's got to be a message of some kind on it!"

"You mean there's a computer in it?" Brady interrupted. "Like *Knight Rider*?"

"I don't know what that means," Petra answered, frowning at the reference.

"TV show," Nate told her. "The car has a talking computer. Artificial intelligence."

As they passed by, they could see shattered windows and dents on the sides and front.

"What happened?" Brady asked.

"We got caught in a *Parasaurolophus* herd," Petra said, staring not at the car but at the ten-foot bank above it. "Knocked us over the edge. We barely got out alive."

For the next half hour, Brady peppered her with questions about future computers and cars, which Petra refused to answer. Finally, Petra pointed. "There." On the bank was a spot that seemed high enough to be suitable for a bonfire.

The only problem was, there was a sauropod dinosaur on top of it.

MAX

WE HIKED ALONG THE RIVERBANK FOR A COUPLE OF HOURS BEFORE we decided we needed to stop and make some kind of campsite for the night. Along the way, we hadn't seen any more of the *T. rex*, just small theropods and an ornithopod or two. I even spotted this thing that looked like a possum that I thought might be an *Alphadon*. I didn't spend too much time rubbernecking, though, because I still didn't really trust Mildred, no matter what she said.

Before too long, we found a rise overlooking the river, about twenty feet up. A lot of sickly-looking ferns formed a meadow that gave way to a bunch of trees, evergreens mixed with trees with leaves. A couple were magnolias, and there were also a few ginkgoes.

We gathered wood and I started a fire. As it blazed comfortably, I pulled the alligator out of my backpack.

Mildred watched, then asked blandly, "I don't suppose you know how to dress it, do you?"

"You do?" I asked. Despite the fact that she could throw a

knife and use a Colt revolver, she seemed sort of prim and not really the type who would've learned things like how to gut an alligator. Of course, I had no clue myself.

"My father hunted. When he brought home a kill, it was my job, and my mother's, to prepare it."

"Even alligator?" I asked.

"If it has four limbs, it's basically all the same."

I hesitated. It wasn't that I didn't think she would do a good job. It's that gutting the thing would require a knife and I wasn't sure I trusted her with one. She could throw them, after all. Not all that accurately, really, but we weren't that far apart right now.

"If you're afraid to give me the knife, I could give directions," she said.

"That would be lovely," I told her, in the same tone. She didn't react.

The creature was torpid but still alive. I dispatched it by thrusting the knife through the back of its neck.

"Turn it over," Mildred said, "and make one long cut, from the neck to the belly." As I did so, she continued. "Really, we should probably eat the liver, but I would wager you're the sort of city boy who's a bit squeamish about such things."

I was, but I wasn't about to tell her that. I opened up the gator and pulled out some of the innards, proffering something red and squishy to her.

"That would be a lung," Mildred said.

When she didn't say anything else, I cut out the rest of the guts and tossed them far into the river. I didn't want them attracting anything that might decide we looked good to eat too.

Then, at Mildred's direction, I rinsed the gator off with water from the canteen and placed it in the embers of the fire.

"Give it about an hour."

By then, I was starving and the sun had gone down. In the distance, I could hear cries of creatures in the night. The glow of the fire and the smoke from damp branches kept the insects away, though. At least, I kept telling myself that.

I cleaned my hands and the knife in the river and filled the canteen. When I returned, I made sure Mildred was across the fire from me. In sight and out of arm's reach.

For a moment, I said nothing, just trying to figure her out. From a certain point of view, her trying to avenge her father's death wasn't all that unreasonable. When I found out my dad had been killed in Afghanistan, I'd been mad for weeks. Of course, my dad wasn't a psycho kidnapper and would-be murderer like hers was.

"I'm sorry about your father," I told her. "I know what it's like to lose your dad. But what happened was – "

"I'm not going to kill you tonight," she said.

"That's . . . reasonable," I said. The fact that she kept telling me she wasn't going to kill me was sort of unnerving. I stared at her across the fire for a moment and decided I believed her. And that

it was safe to dry my shoes. Being here without footwear could be fatal. I opened up the laces and set my shoes close to the fire. "Don't steal my stuff, either."

She looked offended. "I'm not a petty thief."

"Look," I said, getting angry now myself. "I get that you're mad and grieving and whatever, and I'm sorry your dad is dead, but he *was* trying to kill me and Mad Jack, and he kidnapped my sister!"

Mildred held up her hand. "Whatever you believe about my father's motivations is manifestly incorrect. But I'm willing to put my feelings aside for the moment. As long as we can be helpful to each other. Do we have a deal?"

"Sure," I replied after a moment. "We have a deal." Whatever.

We were silent for a while. I wondered where Petra and Brady and Nate were, hoped that they were all on the boat and that it was okay. There had been a lot of *Deinosuchus* around when we'd last spotted the boat, and one of them could've mistaken it for dinner. Or maybe not mistaken.

And that led me to wondering what Emma and Kyle were doing with Uncle Nate. My brother and sister could take care of themselves, mostly, but I was beginning to realize I didn't know Uncle Nate as well as I thought.

I prayed they were all safe.

I hadn't realized that that much time had gone by when

Mildred used a stick to pull the gator from the fire. A succulent aroma rose from the carcass. She gestured. "Bon appétit."

The gator needed salt or maybe cayenne pepper, but it was hot and good.

As I gnawed on a piece of the tail, I stared at Mildred for a moment across the fire.

"Do you have a question?"

"What do you know about all this?" I asked. "I mean, really know?"

"I know," she answered, "that time travel is not to be trifled with. And that I wish to return home." She nibbled delicately on a chunk of a leg, chewed, and swallowed. "Are you going to slit *my* throat in the night?"

I coughed. My first impulse was to say no, but I choked it back. "Probably not."

"What happened with your father?" she asked after a moment. "How did he die?"

"He was in the military," I answered slowly, not just because I didn't really like to talk about it. "And I'm not sure I should say anything more. Because of that whole space-time-continuum issue."

Which sounded sort of ridiculous when I said it aloud.

"Fair enough. You take the first watch, then," she said. "Good night."

With that, she took a couple of steps from the fire and lay down, her back to me, on a pile of fern fronds she'd arranged earlier.

I finished off my portion of the gator, then tossed the rest of the remains into the river and sat, my back to a tree, near the fire. I took a sip of water and attempted to relax, listening to the forest noises, trying to stay awake, thoughts drifting.

And they kept circling. My first thought was that I didn't really want to die here and that it really was kind of easy to kill a person if you didn't care about the mess. You could do it with a gun, a knife, a rock, a loaf of bread, a bowl of sugar, or a *Tyrannosaurus rex*.

Which led me back to the same thing: Brady was going to die. Unless I told him. But maybe I had told him and he went anyway, and what if I wrecked the entire space-time continuum? Okay, that last worry didn't seem all that likely, but it wasn't irrelevant. Yes, Mildred was right. Time travel was, or could be, dangerous. We didn't really *know*.

I didn't know why it was bugging me so much. Samuel was dead and it hadn't weirded me out to know him. But at least in our time, he'd lived a full life.

Brady hadn't. Assuming he made it back, at age thirty he would be in a building outside Houston constructed so people could take time off and have fun, and instead it killed them.

< 116 >

Dozens of people were going to live because of him, but he'd be dead.

It wasn't just a space-time-continuum issue, though. If I were in Brady's position, I didn't know if I'd want someone to tell me the day I was going to die.

I stared at the fire long into the night.

NATE

"THAT'S, LIKE, A *BRONTOSAURUS*, RIGHT?" NATE ASKED, ADJUSTING his glasses. "Or one of those things we're not supposed to call a *Brontosaurus* anymore? That Fred Flintstone used as a crane at the quarry?"

Despite its long neck and long tail, it was small, no more than about twenty feet long from nose to tail and maybe six feet tall at the shoulder. It had a grayish-green lizard-like hide and it was grazing on ferns.

"No, it's not *Apatosaurus*. *Alamosaurus*, maybe," Brady answered, staring up at the long-necked creature. "Juvenile."

"And you want us to go up there?" Nate said to Petra. "How much does this dinosaur weigh? A couple tons?"

"Probably," she answered. She pulled an arrow from her quiver and nocked it.

"Hold on," Brady said. Reaching over, he turned the ignition key. The outboard motor roared to life, startling the *Alamosaurus*. When Brady revved the engine, the creature glanced our way and then trundled off, back into the forest of redwoods beyond.

"Nice," Petra murmured.

Brady wrapped the anchor line around a cypress tree and the trio climbed up the riverbank, Nate nearly passing out as his leg banged a tree root on the way. From where they stood, a good fifteen feet up from the water level and maybe ten feet or so higher than the surrounding bank, the bonfire would be in clear view from the river and the other bank.

Nate rested while Petra and Brady spent the next couple of hours gathering wood for the signal fire. They thought that it would also keep predators at bay and, possibly, help with the mosquitoes. The problem with all those nature documentaries, Nate decided, was that they never covered the insect problem.

Finally, they had enough wood for the bonfire and used it to form a tepee shape about six feet high. They also set up the hibachi off to the side, where Petra told the boys she would cook the hadrosaur.

Nate wasn't sure when she'd decided she was in charge, but since neither he nor Brady had ever cooked a dinosaur before, they went with it.

"It'll be dark in about an hour," Petra said. "Let's get dinner ready first, and then we can light the bonfire."

Using a flint and steel, Petra got the cook fire going a lot quicker than Brady or Nate would've. Once it burned down, she used one of the hunting knives to slice the hadrosaur leg into a couple of pieces vaguely resembling brisket and placed them on the rack. The rest of the leg she tossed into the river. The meat was a dark pink, not quite as red as beef, but more red than pork.

Then she cut off a couple of dime-size pieces and set them down in front of Aki. The little dromaeosaur took one sniff and then scurried over underneath a fern and began digging in the dirt. He dislodged some kind of beetle and pounced, crunching it down with dinosaurian glee.

Not long after that, as the trees became shadows, the group lit the bonfire.

In its light, they pulled out the hadrosaur meat.

"Not bad," Brady said as he gnawed.

"Could use some salt, though," Nate replied.

"Oh, here," Petra told them, pulling salt and pepper shakers from her pocket.

"Where'd you get these?" Nate asked, just as he drew the obvious conclusion.

She shrugged. "Mad Jack's cottage. He had an entire spice rack in one cabinet. I didn't bring any others, though."

The seasonings helped. A lot. The texture and flavor of the *Kritosaurus* was kind of halfway between beef and pork, just like the color. And salt was always good.

"How did you learn to do this sort of thing?" Nate asked. "Fires. Shooting dinosaurs. Cooking dinosaurs. Most girls . . . don't."

Brady kicked his brother. "Are you going to tell Ernie that, or should I?"

Nate turned red. Brady was right. Ernie camped and fished and hunted as much as he and Brady did. Not as well as Petra, though.

Petra laughed. "You live in the country. I'm betting most girls there . . . do."

Nate turned even redder.

That's when he remembered — not that he'd ever really forgotten — that she lived on the ranch. Their ranch. That she knew their father.

"What's he like?" Nate asked. He nodded at Brady. "Our father, I mean. Is he still crazy obsessed about time travel? And a reclusive lunatic?"

Brady went rigid at his brother's last remark but didn't dispute what he said.

Petra's expression didn't change. She held out her hand to Aki, who came over and took a piece of meat from her. "I like your dad." Then she sighed. "But, yeah, sometimes he drives my mom crazy. And I hope he makes it."

Brady held up a hand. "Wait. What?"

Petra grimaced but continued. "My mom's his nurse, house-keeper, and pretty much takes care of him. And I probably shouldn't be telling you all this."

"No," Nate said. "That wasn't what I was asking about."

"I know. For the last few years, my mom and I have been just about the only people he's seen." Petra hesitated, then crossed her legs underneath herself. "Just after Kyle, Emma, and Max arrived for the summer, and just before we came here, your father had a heart attack."

Nate stared. "Are you saying that in thirty years or whatever, he's still going to be the same crazy-obsessed whackjob?"

Petra didn't answer. She just picked at the leaves of a fern frond.

Nate jumped up and took two steps into the forest before deciding that anger and outrage weren't an excuse to go blundering into a *Tyrannosaurus rex*. He turned, ignoring Brady's snort, and clambered, half falling, down the cliff to the bass boat.

It rocked in the water as he stepped over and threw himself sideways into a seat. He just sat there and, well, sulked.

A few minutes later, his brother came down the bank and stood in front of him.

Before Brady could speak, Nate started to vent. "What is *wrong* with him? He doesn't take care of himself, he does stupid things, and he's never, ever there . . ."

"Petra says . . ." Brady began. "Petra says he closed off the ranch because they — we — found some fossil footprints."

"So?" Nate said. "There are all kinds of dinosaur tracks on the ranch."

"But these were from a human girl."

Nate's eyes widened. "What?"

"Emma, Max's sister, left them. It's how they knew how to find her."

Nate frowned. "But that still doesn't explain why Dad's so obsessed about the Chronal Engine in *our* time. He doesn't know about the footprints yet, does he?"

Brady just shrugged. "Maybe he has a reason for what he's doing now, the same way he'll have a reason for closing off the ranch then."

Nate gave up. He adjusted his glasses and sat up straight, feet on the floor of the boat.

"Oh." He adjusted his legs. "Why?"

"I don't know," Brady answered. "I told you."

"No," Nate said. "Why are my feet wet?" When he'd put them down, they'd splashed into water. Sure, there'd been a little of it from when the *Deinosuchus* had nearly capsized them, but this was deep. Several inches deep.

Nate jumped up and perched on the back of the seat. "We're sinking!"

MAX

IN THE MORNING, I AWOKE NOT DEAD. IT FELT KIND OF GOOD TO realize I hadn't been knifed in my sleep by Mildred or disemboweled by a stray dromaeosaur. On the other hand, I really hadn't slept all that well because I'd been afraid of being knifed in my sleep by Mildred or disemboweled by a stray dromaeosaur. It did mean, though, that Mildred kept her word. Unless she was trying to lull me into a false sense of complacency.

The fire had burned down to embers, and Mildred was asleep beside it, even though it was her watch. I let her lie while I stood and walked over to the riverbank. We hadn't seen the others or heard the bass boat during the night. At least I hadn't. I'd doubted they'd have traveled in the dark, anyway. In all probability, they were downriver on their way to the launch, hoping for us to catch up.

But that meant we had another problem, which I hadn't mentioned yet to Mildred: we were on the wrong side of the river.

But I had had an idea last night.

I sat on the edge of the riverbank next to a pair of palmettos, my legs dangling over the side. Birds called in the trees in the meadow behind me. Below, I saw piles of driftwood that had ended up on the bank in the bow of the river. The dry ones would be useful for what I had in mind.

Along the edge of the river, a pair of alvarezsaurs — two-legged feathered theropods, about two feet tall — waded, occasionally darting their heads into the water to pick up a fish or maybe a mollusk of some kind. They had tiny, stubby arms that ended in hands with a single finger and claw. Paleontologists had debated for years whether they were dinosaurs or birds and what they used those weird claws for. And now, seeing the alvarezsaurs in person, I still didn't have a clue. "Ahh, science."

"What about science?" Mildred asked. As I turned, she sat up, brushed the dirt and leaves off her safari garb, and stood.

"Nothing," I replied. She came over to stand beside me. "Have you ever built a raft?"

Her expression didn't change. "Why?"

"The steamboat will be on the other side of the river," I told her. I paused. "And I haven't seen a *Deinosuchus* since yesterday, but I don't really think I want to try *swimming* across."

Not that going by raft would be that much safer, but . . .

Mildred was silent a moment. "If we continue farther downriver, we'll eventually reach the sea, and crossing at the mouth could expose us to dangerous currents and antediluvian sea creatures."

"Exactly," I told her.

It took most of the morning. We used eight or so logs about six inches in diameter for the main body of the raft, lashed together with vines we cut down from the trees along the meadow. I used another log as an outrigger, attaching it with poles to the main part of the raft.

The vessel ended up being about eight feet long and four feet wide, not counting the outrigger.

"Do you see any of the alligators?" Mildred asked as we prepared to launch.

"No," I replied. "But look." A ways upriver, on the far side, was a hadrosaur carcass. A trio of small feathered dromaeosaurs was atop it, squeaking and tearing out tiny chunks of flesh. "If there are any *Deinosuchus*, hopefully they'll go there."

We launched, shoving the raft into the water. Mildred climbed up front and knelt, holding a driftwood paddle to pull us forward. I climbed aboard behind her, hoping we had enough momentum to get us quickly to the other side. The raft sank under our weight, so that our knees were under water by a couple of inches, but we stayed afloat.

"Paddle!" I said, as soon as we were away from the bank. Together, nicely synchronous, we started making headway.

About halfway across, scanning upriver, I spotted a head with a V-shaped wake behind it. It was a *Deinosuchus*, a smallish one, maybe only about seven or eight feet long. But it was heading toward us.

"Move!" I shouted, pointing. Instantly, Mildred plunged her paddle into the water and we picked up the pace, though not nearly as fast as I would've liked. I kept an eye on the alligator. We still had time, I thought, as both the alligator and the shore got closer.

When we were maybe a raft's length from the riverbank, the *Deinosuchus* was only about twenty feet from us and disappeared from view.

"Jump!" I shouted. As soon as I said it, Mildred sprang up and toward the bank.

I raised my paddle up, readied as a spear. At the same instant, the alligator launched itself from the water. I thrust the paddle forward, striking the upturned jaw of the alligator and turning it aside, even as it ripped the paddle from my hand. As the *Deinosuchus* thrashed with the paddle, I jumped to my feet and leaped toward the riverbank, falling half in the water.

I scrambled up the bank, pulled by Mildred, as the raft drifted away in the struggle. Finally, I was on dry land, on my side, legs readied to kick out. I caught a glimpse of Mildred swinging her paddle, and the alligator was gone.

As I lay there, relieved not to be food for a prehistoric reptile, of all things, Mildred stood over me. "Well, then. Shall we proceed?"

After a few minutes to recover and take a drink of water, we headed off, walking along the bank for another hour or two before we reached the sea. The forest of redwoods gave way to a marshy beach. The gleaming white sand was marred only by seaweed at tide level and piles of dung from sauropod dinosaurs, their birdbath-size footprints crisscrossing the sand. We stayed close to the forest because we didn't want to be out in the open if a *T. rex* or its smaller cousin, *Nanotyrannus,* lumbered along.

We came upon the stranded steamboat late in the afternoon, its once-white hull now flaking away.

"I recognize it," Mildred said. "My father has photographs of himself on it with Mad Jack before their falling-out. It's called *Mary Anne.*"

We picked up the pace, almost running along the beach to reach the boat. It lay half buried in the sand, on an angle, a large hole in its hull exposing the lower deck, where the mechanical workings of the boat resided.

"Hello!" I shouted, then flinched as a pair of Quetzalcoatlus swooped low over us, then flew away.

"I've seen them eat beasts the size of large dogs," Mildred said.

"I shuddered, and when the pterosaurs were safely on their way, I picked up a piece of driftwood and struck the hull a couple of times, not because I expected anyone to be there, but because last time, there had been an oviraptorosaur inside.

I didn't hear anything from within the boat, so I circled

around, then peered into the hole. Nothing. I climbed up onto the deck. Back in its day, the launch had had a small cabin cockpit in the rear. Up front, there was an opening in the deck that exposed the steam engine. A now-rusted smokestack rose about ten feet above the deck.

Next to the smokestack stood a box about the size of a microwave oven. I lifted the lid. Inside was a prototype large-scale Recall Device. From what I understood, it had been an early model to see if large objects — like the boat — could be moved through time and space. But it was unwieldy, so Mad Jack designed the handheld baseball-size ones. The maze of wires and conduits underneath the control panel interface glowed green, a promising sign.

I pulled a handwritten note out of the box. One I'd left behind the last time we'd come. It was addressed to Emma, telling her that we were there, that we'd rescue her. I handed it to Mildred. "See?"

She read it without comment while I peered into the workings of the Recall Device.

"Looks like it should still work," I murmured.

"Good," Mildred said.

Something in her tone made me look over at her.

The last thing I saw was a piece of driftwood coming at my head.

CHAPTER
XXIII

NATE

"PETRA!" BRADY YELLED TOWARD THE SHORE. "WE NEED TO GET everything off the boat!"

Her startled face appeared at the edge of the bank.

"Stay there!" Brady said. "And catch!"

Nate was already opening the compartments and pulling the supplies onto the deck, ignoring the pain in his leg. He tossed up cans of peas and beans while Brady threw the tackle box. Past Petra, not *at* Petra.

Before they finished, the boat had settled to the bottom of the river, with just the windshield peeking above the water.

Glumly, they gathered everything they could and put it in a pile by the fire.

Sunrise came while Nate was on watch. They'd kept the fire going for around three hours, but there was no sign of Max and Mildred.

Brady lay sleeping on his back next to Nate, while Petra was asleep on her side by the fire, her bow and the quiver of arrows beside her. Aki rested behind her neck.

Nate stood and stretched, wincing as stabs of pain shot through his leg. At his movement, Aki got up and began hunting in the ferns. Nate tried to track him, but the dromaeosaur almost immediately disappeared from view and Nate didn't want to follow.

Instead, he limped over to stand at the river's edge. He didn't see any gators, but on the other side was a flock of things that looked like ostriches, but with long reptile tails and arms instead of wings. They were about the size of ostriches too, but had blue and red feathers on their bodies and green necks. They milled about in the shallows, clucking and drinking from the river.

Nate nudged his brother awake with his foot. Brady blinked and groaned but then stared where Nate pointed.

"Ornithomimids," Brady said. "Ostrich mimics." Then he did a double take. "And they do have feathers!"

As he began talking about what an earth-shattering discovery this was for paleontology and our understanding of dinosaur and bird evolution, Nate tossed another log onto the campfire and they woke Petra.

The first thing they did was try to make breakfast, but they soon realized they'd left the can opener on the boat. So, leaving his shoes and socks on the riverbank, Brady climbed down to the boat to fetch the opener from the cockpit.

"Any way we can get the boat out of the water?" Petra asked.

"If we could repair the leak and had a bilge pump, maybe,"

Brady said. He lifted the motor to check again where the *Deinosuchus* had attacked. "There's a hole."

At the base of the stern, right behind the motor, the gator had punctured the boat, creating a hole about the size of a dime that had slowly filled the boat with water. Maybe back home they could've hauled it back up on its trailer and repaired it, but here, for now, the boat was a goner.

After a meal of peas and potatoes, they headed out, leaving behind most of the cans (too heavy and awkward to carry) but bringing the tackle box with its hooks and line.

"You know," Brady said as he hefted the box, "fishing is so much easier with dynamite."

"Next time I'm at the Piggly Wiggly I'll be sure to pick some up," Petra said in the same tone.

"Oh, shut up," Nate told them both.

MAX

I AWOKE TO A SHARP PAIN IN MY HAND AND A WORSE ONE IN MY head. I felt the bump above my ear and groaned, swearing at myself for having let my guard down around Mildred. At least when I brought my hand down to check, there wasn't any blood. Rolling over onto my side, I wiped sand off my face and then froze when something screeched in my ear.

As my vision cleared and I blinked more sand out of my eyes, I got a good look at the creature that had pecked my hand and was making the really annoying sound. It was an oviraptorosaur: bipedal, feathered, with a beak like a parrot's and a weird crest like a rooster's. Its markings were like a parrot's too, green on the body with red highlights on the feathered arms. It was about five feet tall and sort of proportioned like an emu. There were three more behind it.

To my left, where the steamboat should've been, was a large damp hole in the sand. Hermit crabs, I guessed, and snails that had been living under the hull were emerging or trying to bury themselves. Three of the oviraptorosaurs were pouncing, jabbing at the crabs with their beaks, cracking shells or swallowing their prey whole.

Paleontologists had suspected their diet might have included invertebrates. I would've been happy that what I was seeing confirmed that theory, except for the pounding in my head and the fact that the absence of the boat meant I was really, truly trapped here alone.

Resisting the urge to throw up, I sat, leaning one hand — the unpecked one — on my backpack. The oviraptorosaur in front of me screeched again, then lowered its head and spread its wings. Raising my arms, I let out the Tarzan yell, which Uncle Nate had taught me how to do when I was five.

This spooked all four of them. They dashed off about ten feet and then turned around. All of them were in the same challenge position now: heads lowered, wings outstretched.

"Really, guys," I said, "I am in no mood."

The lead oviraptorosaur gave a quizzical squawk but otherwise didn't react.

Then I realized Mildred had left me my backpack.

For a moment, I sat there, then opened it up on the smooth sand. Out of the corner of my eye, without turning my head, I noticed the oviraptorosaurs had apparently decided I wasn't a threat and had gone back to digging for crabs.

I pulled out the first-aid kit to grab an aspirin. As I unzipped the pouch, the USB flash drive fell out onto the sand.

"All right, why did you give me this?" I murmured.

It couldn't have been an accident, but Uncle Nate and Kyle had to have known I didn't have anything to plug it into or play it on. Mad Jack Pierson hadn't left anything useful either, since his equipment was mostly vacuum tubes and cogs and sprockets. There wasn't anything here, except . . .

"Yes!" I jumped to my feet and then swayed, dizzy. But I was okay enough to let out a whoop, holding the flash drive tightly in my fist. "A late-model Volkswagen Beetle with a USB accessory port and built-in dashboard entertainment and navigation system!" I let out another whoop despite the fact that the last one had made my head hurt.

In response, the oviraptorosaurs chirped and then fled completely.

I didn't care. I had a way home. At least, the potential for one. I had to make it up the river to the car and hope its electrical system still functioned.

But at least now I had a chance.

I grabbed my backpack, hoisted it over my shoulders, and headed inland.

It didn't take me long to get back to the river, and I followed it into the redwood forest. I was basically retracing the route I had taken with Petra and Emma in the VW the first time we'd come here. I hoped that I'd be able to spot the bass boat and get a ride from Petra and my uncles.

It wasn't a good sign, though, that they weren't here. I tried not to think of the many things that could have happened to them. That could still happen to them. Or me.

I hiked up the river for a few hours until I came upon a shallow creek that was crowded by mossy rocks and logs, with ferns and horsetails growing close to the water's edge. The creek was about six feet wide and no more than six inches deep. Splashing through the water, I went about thirty feet upstream to get clear of where the water from the creek mixed with the river. Then my way was blocked by a rotting, moss-covered redwood — about four feet in diameter — that lay across the creek, a couple of feet above the level of the water.

I took a break, sitting on another log half-buried in the bank, refilling my canteen and cooling off.

After a few minutes, I heard an odd snuffling noise, like a pig with a head cold. I stood, trying to figure out where it was coming from. Then I saw a creature coming into view, emerging from the forest along the creek about halfway between me and the river.

It was an *Ankylosaurus*. Or maybe a *Euoplocephalus*. It was about five feet tall and at least as wide, with an armored trapezoidal head held close to the ground, spikes along its side and armor plates over its back. A huge club at the end of its tail was swinging from side to side.

They were herbivores, but the creature's beak looked like it could just as easily tear flesh. Slowly, so as not to spook it, I stepped along the fallen redwood trunk, intending to cross the creek and go around the ankylosaur.

But it saw me and bleated, swinging its tail club so that it thudded into a tree beside it. I froze as the dinosaur took a ponderous step toward me. And then another.

I dived to the ground — into the creek, actually — and rolled under the redwood log. I could hear the animal's bleat above my splashing of the water, but I made it to the other side of the fallen trunk without the creature charging me. I rose, dripping, watching the ankylosaur from the relative safety of my side of the log. Then, satisfied the dinosaur wasn't going to try to come after me, I turned and saw, about fifteen feet away, watching me watching the ankylosaur, a pair of *Nanotyrannus*. Like *Tyrannosaurus rex*, only smaller — about six feet high at the hip — and with a lighter build. I dived back under the log and scrambled across the creek beneath it. At the edge, I glanced to my right and saw that the *Nanotyrannus* had gotten closer, but they seemed more interested in the ankylosaur than me.

The armored dinosaur hadn't moved, so I crawled out from beneath the trunk, sprang onto dry ground, and ran without looking back.

I was still running, heading away from the dinosaurs and sort of parallel to the river, when I rounded a redwood and collided with someone.

Brady.

He went down like he'd been hit in the head with a baseball bat, and I tumbled on top of him. Nate and Petra were there too, just beyond. For a moment, we all froze.

"Sorry," I muttered to Brady as I stood and reached out a hand.

Before he answered, Petra squealed and embraced me in a hug. Which was nice.

"I am so glad to see you!" she said, smiling and kissing me on the cheek. Which was also nice. Then she stepped back. "I'm so glad I don't have to tell Kyle and your sister you're dead." Which was less nice.

"Never mind me," Brady said. "Yes, I'm okay."

Nate and I helped him to his feet and he made a show of dusting himself off.

Nate asked, "Where's Mildred?"

I grimaced. "She clubbed me, then stole the steamboat."

"Stole the steamboat," Brady repeated, glancing up.

"So she took the only Recall Device?" Petra asked, eyes widening. "What now?"

"I have an idea," I said, reaching into my backpack to pull out the first-aid pouch.

"The USB drive!" Petra exclaimed. "The VW!"

"I know!" I said. "There's got to be something on this we can use to get home. It's the only explanation that makes sense!"

"So, back the way we came?" Nate asked with a sigh.

"The walk'll do you good," his brother told him.

We made it to the VW by midafternoon.

The Bug was dented and the glass was shattered, but its front end — which meant its engine — was sticking mostly out of the water. I climbed down to look, while the others remained on the top of the bank. It was late enough in the afternoon that the interior was completely shadowed and it was hard to see. Even though I knew it was ludicrous, I tried not to think about my nightmare of plunging into an abyss. This car had already fallen. There was nothing to worry about, I told myself. Except, of course, the possibility that the car wouldn't start.

Thankfully Kyle had left the key in the ignition, so we wouldn't need to hotwire it or anything. I didn't need the engine to work, just the electrical system. Since it had been only a few days since we'd left it here, the battery should still be good. Of course, that assumed only a few days had gone by in this time period, too.

I turned the key so that the accessories would trigger. Instantly, the dashboard lights went on and the video screen lit up.

"Yes!" I shouted up to the others. "It works!"

I pulled the flash drive out of my pocket as the car shifted slightly. When I looked up, Brady was balanced on the outside of the car, peering in through the side window.

"Hi, Brady," I said.

"This," he replied, "I had to see."

I had a brief moment of concern about what was on the drive and whether he should see his brother's future self, but then I decided it was more important that we get out of there. I plugged the USB drive into the port. At first, there was nothing. Then a video appeared on the monitor. And out of the speakers came track 7 from the soundtrack to the movie *Jurassic Park*, "Welcome to Jurassic Park."

"This is *much* better than *Knight Rider*," Brady said.

Kyle's face appeared.

"It's my brother," I murmured, for Brady's benefit, and then to the screen: "What have you been doing in England?"

"Hello, baby brother," Kyle said. "From what Uncle Nate says, you lost your Recall Device and you're going to need a little help getting home.

"It turns out that Nate and Brady also lost a Recall Device. Very careless of you all, by the way. But *theirs* is still back there in the Cretaceous and you're going to have to go fetch it."

"It's at the bottom of a swamp!" Brady interjected.

"Theirs," video Kyle continued, "is at the bottom of a lake. So here's the thing. You're going to use the canoe from the dogtrot to get out there. The problem is that visibility is poor and you

don't have GPS to find the thing. So you're going to have to tri-angulate."

An animated map appeared on the screen. It looked a bit like a Google Earth view, but not as real. "Uncle Nate made this using coordinates from the Chronal Engine—don't ask me how, and don't blame me if it isn't one hundred percent accurate."

"Does that look right?" I asked Brady.

"Maybe," he replied, leaning in. "I was a bit too busy to play cartographer. Are all cars like this in your time?"

Four trees became highlighted in red. "These are the four biggest trees in close proximity," video Kyle said. He looked over his shoulder. "The four biggest angiosperms. Among other things, that means they have leaves, not needles, and aren't ginkgoes. You shouldn't have any problem figuring out which ones they are."

Then lines connected opposite pairs to form an X. "Use fishing line to make the lines. There should be some in the tackle box from the bass boat."

"X marks the spot where the boat trailer landed," he continued. "The Recall Device is lying next to the right rear tire of the trailer."

The view shifted to an image of the Chronal Engine itself, in Grandpa's basement.

"You're probably wondering why we haven't just come to get you," Kyle continued.

"Well, yes," Brady murmured.

"Uncle Nate is worried about the number of Recall Devices in play," Kyle said. "Actually, not the number, really, but the fact that each Recall Device may be being used during different times, and keeping track of that and the mass . . . stresses the system. The Chronal Engine itself.

"So grab the one at the bottom of the lake. Make sure you dry it out. And then come back here.

"And by 'here,' I mean the ranch, not Uncle Nate's flat in London."

With that, the video ended, an image of the map remaining on the screen.

"Does that make sense?" I asked Brady, who was still staring down at me from above. "You recognize this place?"

"We'll be out of here in no time," he replied. Then he lifted an eyebrow. "So my brother can get back to his flat in London."

CHAPTER XXV

NATE

AFTER THAT, THEY HIKED FOR AN HOUR OR SO BEFORE BRADY declared that he was starving and dead tired and suggested they stop for the night. Nate, who had been straggling behind, limping as his leg throbbed, didn't object, although he knew the others could've continued for hours more.

They made camp next to a cluster of cypresses on a rise about ten feet above the river, a bank too high for *Deinosuchus* to climb. Almost as soon as they got the fire started, Nate fell asleep.

In the morning, when he awoke, Petra and Max were asleep, and Brady was sitting across the fire from him, tapping a twig on the ground, playing with Aki.

"You didn't wake me for my watch," Nate said, sitting up.

"You needed the sleep more," Brady told him. Nate didn't like to be coddled, but he had to admit his brother was right. Nate felt slightly better for the rest, but still feverish and not all that great. He peered down at his leg. The bites were starting to scab a little, but they were oozing more than Nate thought was healthy.

After a quick breakfast of energy bars and a can of baked beans, the foursome was on the march again. Petra took the lead with Max behind her. Brady went next, while Nate limped along at the rear. His leg was throbbing now with every step.

After about an hour, as Petra and Max crossed a narrow stream, Brady looked back, watching Nate as he caught up. "Nate, you look terrible."

"I'm fine," he replied, gritting his teeth.

Turning, Brady called out, "Petra, Max, slow down! Nate's having trouble with his leg."

"Gee, thanks," Nate murmured.

Ahead, Petra didn't answer. She was staring at something in a clearing beyond, her bow raised, an arrow at the ready.

Brady and Nate closed the distance to take in the scene. A moss-covered redwood stump stood about four feet tall in the middle of the clearing. The decayed remains of the rest of the tree lay sprawled in the distance, half buried in the soil beneath ferns and undergrowth.

"Stay very still," Petra said. "We're downwind, at least."

Some kind of two-legged dinosaur, sort of stocky and about eight or ten feet long, maybe four feet high at the hip, with scaly gray and black skin and a strange bald head that looked like a monk's tonsure, stood in front of the log, bleating. Flecks of blood streaked its flanks. Surrounding it were four other bipedal dinosaurs, each one feathered, with sharp teeth and claws. They looked sort of like eagles, but with clawed hands rather than wings, and mouths with sharp teeth, not beaks.

"Pachycephalosaur," Brady said, pointing to the injured dinosaur. "The other guys are dromaeosaurs of some kind. *Deinonychus*, maybe."

"The pachycephalosaur's probably *Texacephale*," Max put in. "But we're about thirty million years too late for *Deinonychus*."

The feathered dinosaurs were about the same height and length as the *Texacephale*, but much more lightly built. They were more lithe, too, and would occasionally jump at the pachycephalosaur's side, digging in with their clawed feet and then scampering away.

"They're about the right size, though," Brady said. "For *Deinonychus*, I mean."

Max nodded. "They could be something like *Richardoestesia*, which we only have teeth for."

The *Texacephale* took a step, let out a shrill cry, and then fell, weak from loss of blood, Nate figured. As soon as it did, the dromaeosaurs pounced and began gorging.

"Let's get out of here," Petra said. With her arrow still aimed toward the feeding pack, she led the way around the edge of the clearing, trying to keep out of sight of the dromaeosaurs.

"Those aren't Aki's species, are they?" Brady asked.

"No," Max answered. "Aki's species is smaller. More like a true *Dromaeosaurus*. Or *Saurornitholestes*."

As the others continued ahead, Nate paused, leaning against a tree, his leg throbbing, watching the pack feed.

Then, to his right, he felt rather than heard something in the forest. As he turned toward it, Petra shouted, "Nate, don't move!"

Then he heard a bowstring snap and the whisper of an arrow in flight. An instant later, there was a thud, and from behind the tree next to him, a dromaeosaur pitched forward onto the ground.

Nate took one step toward the others, and then another, and then a searing pain shot through his leg and he fell on his face, glasses flying to the ground.

The others rushed over. Max handed him a canteen while Brady picked up the glasses.

Nate gulped the water as Brady put the back of his hand to his brother's forehead. "Fever."

Then Brady opened Nate's glasses and, to Nate's embarrassment, put them back on his face.

"Let's get going." Nate tried to stand, but his leg wouldn't cooperate. As he sagged against the others, he told them, "You're going to have to leave me here."

"That's crazy," Brady said.

"Absolutely," Max said.

Petra pulled her arrow from the body of the dromaeosaur and gave the two of them a quizzical look. "A stretcher, maybe?"

Brady shook his head. "A travois."

CHAPTER
XXVI

MAX

"WHAT'S A TRAVOIS?" I ASKED.

Brady pulled the machete from its scabbard and gestured. "It's almost the same thing as a stretcher, but you let one end drag on the ground. French trappers used them in precolonial days. They got the idea from the Plains Indians."

It turned out to be easier to build than the raft — just a couple of stout poles and a bunch of crossbars. We got it finished in next to no time, rigging it so that most of the weight would be borne at the shoulders using the straps from the backpack, instead of by the handles. Brady took the first go, dragging his brother behind.

After a couple of hours, we switched off and I took over the pulling. It was harder than I wanted it to be but a bit easier than I expected. Wheels would've been helpful, though they might actually sink into the ground, and we had to lift the travois over fallen logs, anyway.

As we hiked along, Brady came up beside me, while Petra walked a few paces ahead, checking out the route.

"So, what happens to me?" he asked.

"What do you mean?" I said, not really wanting an answer. I wondered if he did either.

"Well, for one thing," he said, "I guess I don't have a flat in London."

I winced and tried to cover it by looking down at my feet to step over a rock.

Brady went on. "You call my brother 'Nate,' but sometimes you slip up and call him 'Uncle Nate.' Me you always call 'Brady' or avoid talking to me at all. Which says to me that you don't know me or you don't know me as your uncle." He took a deep breath. "So, the thing is, do I make it out of here?"

I was silent a long time, trying to decide what to say. Finally, I answered. "Yes."

"But I was right: You don't know me, do you?" Brady pursued.

There was no good answer, no good thing to do here. After another long pause, during which he never took his eyes off me, I replied. "I don't know you. But that's all I can tell you."

"Hey," he said, "we're family."

"I'm sorry," I mumbled. "I can't tell you."

NATE

IT WASN'T A COMFORTABLE RIDE. NATE COULD FEEL EVERY ROCK AND stick and stick and unevenness in the ground as he was bounced around. Every now and then, something hit his bad leg.

It was almost better when they crossed streams and Nate had to actually get up and wade across, even though he needed Brady's help.

Most of the time, though, he just lay there, thinking. He'd heard what Brady had said to Max and what Max hadn't said to Brady.

Nate still didn't know what the deal was with his father but realized there was something more going on here than he knew. Than any of them knew. They were going to have to have a long family conversation, he decided, when they got back.

"This is it," Max said sometime late that afternoon as he stopped and let down the travois.

Nate got up and turned to look. They had arrived at the top of an arroyo that had a creek running through it. The arroyo wall was higher on the side opposite them and a hill rose beyond that. Set about halfway up the far wall was a cave.

What caught his attention and his brother's, though, was the pair of handmade ladders. One leaned against the terrace at the mouth of the cave, leading up from the creek bed, while another allowed access from the cave to the top of the arroyo.

"You made this?" Nate asked as Max started down the arroyo wall.

"No," Petra answered.

"It was Samuel — your grandfather Samuel," Max said, looking up as Brady handed him the travois. "He was here looking for Mad Jack."

"Did he ever find him?" Brady wanted to know, reaching a hand out to help his brother down the wall.

"I don't know," Max answered.

By the time he made it up to the cave, Nate was sweating from effort, head pounding. He sat leaning against the cave wall while the others built a fire on the cave terrace. He dozed a bit and drank from a canteen while everyone else sat out on the terrace. Every now and then he caught part of a conversation.

"If everything goes well, we should be able to get him to a doctor tomorrow," Max said. He turned to look at Nate. "If it's in your time, there's something you should probably know. That the doctors probably won't."

"What?" Brady asked.

"It might not be just an infection," Max answered. "Mosasaurs might have some kind of venom. Like Komodo dragons."

"You mean the bacteria from their mouths?"

"No," Max replied. "Actual venom. Komodo dragons have been discovered to have poison glands. The stuff about bacterial infections from bad flossing, or whatever, is a myth. But the venom might be why the bites aren't scabbing all that well."

For a moment, there was silence. Then Nate heard Brady say, "You can tell us about that but not about what happens to me?"

Nate didn't hear an answer.

MAX

AFTER A LONG NIGHT, WHICH I SPENT HALF AWAKE TRYING TO DECIDE whether I'd done the right thing by not telling Brady about the stadium collapse, the morning dawned cloudy and dark.

Skipping breakfast, we set out in a light drizzle and made it to the island by midday. To my surprise, we didn't see any dinosaurs. I guess not even the big carnivorous ones like the rain.

After a lunch of another can of baked beans, we readied the canoe. Brady took the front, with Nate in the back. I wasn't really sure Nate should actually be expending that much energy, but he told me that while rowing required the use of the legs, he would just be paddling, which didn't. Since I was going to have to be swimming later to find the Device, I went with it. Petra took the third spot, on the floor of the canoe, and I was between her and Brady. He hadn't said a word to me since the mosasaur conversation.

Midafternoon, we reached the cove where Brady and Nate had splashed down. The rain had continued for most of the morning, the light drizzle graduating to a steady downpour, and the skies didn't look like they were clearing at all. The lake was getting choppy, with waves occasionally sloshing over the sides of the canoe. I crouched, the water pooling around my feet.

"Do you see any mosasaurs?" Nate asked.

"No," I replied. "But I think those are the trees." I pointed as we came around a bend. Two on each side of the lagoon, just like the video Kyle had described.

Nate and Brady rowed us over to the first tree. By then, the waves were choppy enough that the twins had a hard time getting us close. Finally, we banged into the tree and I grabbed on.

"Can you make the shot?" I asked as Petra tied the end of the spool of fishing line to her arrow.

She slid the spool over the end of another arrow and handed it to me. Then she nocked the first and sighted to the tree diagonally across the lake. While the boat bobbed and the wind gusted, she took the shot.

As the arrow arced over the lake, the spool spun on the arrow I was holding and the line unwound. Brady spoke. "Isn't this sort of what Ben Franklin did?"

"That was a kite and a key and lightning," Nate said. "And shut up." A moment later, the arrow thudded into the tree.

"Nice shooting!" I exclaimed as Brady let out a yell of triumph.

I reached up and looped the spool around a thick branch of the tree we were up against, pulling the fishing line tight and tying it off as the waves banged the canoe against the trunk.

"We have to move!" Petra shouted as thunder rumbled in the distance.

"And bail!" Nate yelled.

As Nate and Brady headed over to the next tree, I grabbed the bait bucket and began scooping water from around my feet.

The canoe danced in the waves, and Nate and Brady began having a hard time keeping our course. Finally, with the water in the boat now reaching about three inches, we made it to the next tree. As Petra readied her bow again, there was a flash of lightning and an almost immediate crack of thunder.

"We can't do this now!" she shouted.

I kept bailing. "We have to! If we don't, the Recall Device could get moved by the current or get buried in silt or something!" Besides, at this point, there really didn't seem to be a good option for shelter anyway.

The canoe bobbed in the water, and the waves and the wind flung us toward the tree.

"Watch out!" Brady shouted as we plunged underneath a low branch. Brady was flung from his seat and into me as the canoe became wedged in place.

Using his paddle, he tried to push us away.

"Hold on!" I said. We may have been stuck, but we were also a lot more stable. "Petra, try it now!"

Again, she raised the bow and released the arrow. It sped

across the lake toward the tree. And landed in the water three feet away from it.

She swore. In German. And then in Spanish.

We recoiled the fishing line on its spool and retrieved the arrow.

Again, Petra nocked it and aimed. For a moment, she was still, almost not breathing. Then she let the arrow loose. This time, it hit the tree dead on.

"Yes!" Petra exclaimed, pumping her fist.

I tied the other end of the line to the tree by us and then helped Brady get the canoe unstuck. In minutes, we were off toward where the crisscross of the fishing lines marked the spot.

As we moved into position, I slipped overboard, trying not to capsize the canoe. It shifted too quickly, but Petra's weight in the middle kept it from tipping.

I coughed as I swallowed water, and then dived. It was hard to see and deeper than I'd expected. I kicked again, and then my hand struck something hard. It was the frame of the boat trailer. I felt my way along it, trying to figure out where the wheels were. Eventually, I came to the hitch, which meant I'd been going in the wrong direction. But at least I knew where the thing was.

I kicked to the surface to get a breath of air, grabbing on to the side of the canoe.

"It's getting worse," Petra shouted above the rain.

I nodded, then dived back down.

This time, I latched on to the trailer right away and found the right rear tire. Scrabbling through the mud with one hand while I held on to the trailer with the other, my hand brushed something round and smooth. Lungs burning, I grabbed it and pushed off from the lake bed, propelling myself upward.

I surfaced and swam quickly to the canoe, then I handed the Recall Device to Brady and hauled myself over the side with a hand from Petra.

"Good job!" Nate said.

"I guess we didn't see any mosasaurs after all," I said, still breathing heavily.

"I wouldn't say that," Petra answered, gesturing to where I had come up, now about twenty feet away.

A carcass floated on the water, bobbing. Sticking out of it were two arrows.

"Let's get out of here," I said, feeling a sudden chill.

NATE

BY THEN, THE RAIN WAS SO HEAVY THAT IT WAS ALMOST HARDER FOR Nate to see with his glasses than without. The lake was even choppier, tossing the canoe with the waves. He felt ill but couldn't tell if it was from his leg or because of all the bobbing around they were doing.

Shivering from the chill of the rain, leg throbbing, Nate was barely able to sit up. But he was determined to sustain his end of the project.

Resting the paddle across his knees, he wiped his glasses on his T-shirt. It didn't help all that much. "We won't make it back to the island at this rate."

"Let's go ashore here," Max said.

At the front, Brady nodded, and they paddled toward the nearest shore.

As they canoed past a pair of trees standing in the water, Nate saw a shape on the lakeshore, half in and half out of the water. It was a dead *Triceratops*, its three-horned skull being lapped at by the waves. When they drew closer, he could make out deep gouges along its side and a large chunk taken out of its neck.

As the crew pulled around the animal, the canoe was rocked by a wave. Nate tried to compensate, but his paddle slipped out of his hands and the canoe went over, dashing them into the water.

He nearly blacked out from the pain as his leg scraped the side of the boat. He came up coughing for air between the canoe and the shore. Leaning on the boat, he was able to stand, the waist-level water supporting his weight on his good leg. "Everyone okay?"

"Make sure we still have the Recall Device!" Brady pulled himself up from the same side of the canoe.

Petra emerged from the other side. "Where's Aki?"

"Here," Max said as he stood behind Nate. The little dromaeosaur sat cowering in Max's right hand, water dripping from his feathers. He sneezed, shivered to shake off the water, and then hopped to the shore. Max's left hand held tightly to the Recall Device. "Here it is. Come on."

Max led the way out of the water. Petra, still holding her bow, scooped up Aki in the crook of an arm. The dromaeosaur huddled close to her, trying to get warm.

With one arm over Brady's shoulder, Nate followed, slipping only once as Max climbed past the trees. In a moment, they emerged into a clearing of ferns and cycads.

"Can you get us out of here?" Brady asked.

"Yeah." Max crouched, holding the Recall Device up to his face, reading the markings. He twisted something on top and then paused. After a moment, he made another adjustment to the Device.

"It's okay?" Petra asked. "No water damage?"

Max shook his head, still intent on the Recall Device.

Nate leaned back against a tree and wiped his glasses on his shirt again. They were still wet, but when he put them back on, he got a better look at the meadow. To the right, there seemed to be a path formed by trampled ferns. He grabbed a downed branch and used it as a crutch, taking a couple of steps closer. When he paused, holding a hand out against another tree, he saw enormous footprints in the mud, leading away from the lakeshore.

At Brady's glance, Nate asked, "What has giant, three-toed feet?"

"How giant?" Brady replied with a frown.

"Yea big," Nate said, balancing on one foot to hold his hands about a yard apart.

"*That*." Petra fluidly nocked an arrow and raised her bow to aim at a *Tyrannosaurus rex*. A big one. It had to have been about twenty feet high, and it was staring right at them.

Slowly, Nate limped back toward the others. He felt the *Tyrannosaurus rex*'s eyes watching him, but it didn't move.

"Doesn't matter." Max stood, glancing over at the giant

predator. "We are outta here now." He held the Recall Device out in front of him with one hand and, with the other, casually pressed the button on top.

And nothing happened.

The *Tyrannosaurus rex* took a step toward them.

Max hit the button again. This time, there was a sizzling sound, and the *Tyrannosaurus* paused.

Then there was a burst of light and a popping sound.

"Ow!" Max yelled. At the same time, Nate heard an arrow leave Petra's bow.

When Nate's eyes cleared from the flash, he saw Max shaking his now-empty hand.

"Uh-oh," Petra said. The *Tyrannosaurus* growled, an arrow stuck in its jaw.

"Where's the Recall Device?" Brady demanded, crouching, pushing aside knee-high ferns on the ground in front of Max.

"It left! On its own!" Max said.

The *Tyrannosaurus* roared and charged.

MAX

"INTO THE TREES!" I YELLED. TOGETHER, BRADY AND I HALF DRAGGED, half carried Nate into a thicket of conifers, their trunks one to two feet in diameter, spaced too close for the *T. rex* to follow us through. At least, I hoped. I glanced over my shoulder. Petra was right behind us.

We plowed over ferns and past cycads, and I nearly fell as we came upon a creek bed.

"Where's the *T. rex?*" I asked.

"We're clear!" Brady said, breathing heavily. "It turned back."

Shaking my hand, which still stung from the Recall Device, I looked behind us. "Good."

"What happened?" Petra asked.

I shook my head. "I don't know. Maybe it was the water interfering with the crystals or something."

"So we're stuck here," Brady said.

I took a step out into the creek bed as rain came down harder.

Petra took in a breath. "Don't move."

"It's back," Nate said.

Upstream from us stood a *T. rex.*

"It's not the same one," Petra whispered. She was right. It didn't have one of her arrows sticking out of its jaw. Not that that really mattered.

"Back into the trees." I took a careful step, feeling exhausted and despairing that there was no way we'd be able to get away from the *T. rex* with Nate.

At that moment, there was a flash of light and a booming sound. In the middle of the creek bed, axle deep in water, a Hummer appeared and turned, blocking the giant theropod's path. Grandpa Pierson's Hummer.

The passenger door opened. It was Emma. "Get in!" Beyond her, I could see Kyle at the wheel.

I flung open the rear door and jumped in, the others right behind. As soon as the door closed, Kyle put the Hummer into gear to drive away from the *T. rex.* Before we moved, the dinosaur stepped forward and nudged the side of the SUV with its snout. The entire vehicle shook. Then Kyle turned to Emma. "Do it."

She reached over to a weird-looking contraption on the dashboard. It was a quartet of Recall Devices, mounted in a brass frame, connected together with wires and copper tubing.

An instant later, there was a flash and we were gone.

NATE

THE **SUV** REAPPEARED AT THE RANCH, ON THE DRIVEWAY IN FRONT of the garage. The door was open, the station wagon visible inside.

"We're home," Nate whispered, almost ready to faint with relief. He leaned back and closed his eyes.

And was shocked into opening them when Brady and Max screamed at the same time.

A shadow fell over the car. And then Nate saw an eye the size of a dinner plate peering through the window.

"*T. rex!*" Max's shout was the first coherent thing Nate heard that penetrated his brain.

At almost the same time, Max reached over the seat past his brother to touch a button on the key chain and the Hummer began emitting a loud siren-like noise.

The *Tyrannosaurus* roared, moisture from its breath fogging the window.

"Please let it work, please let it work," Max began muttering as the *Tyrannosaurus* shoved the vehicle again with its snout. The SUV rocked and the window cracked, but the car stayed upright.

"Why isn't it working?" Kyle said, shooting Max an accusing look over his shoulder.

"I don't know!" Max said. "The VW siren . . . maybe it's a different frequency or – "

At that moment, beside the car, there came a snarl and furious barking.

"Thor!" Nate exclaimed, and shoved Brady aside to look out the far window.

The dog was poised beside the car, barking and snarling, confronting the giant dinosaur. Nate had never heard him sound like that.

Brady made a choking sound. "He's going to get eaten."

The *Tyrannosaurus* rumbled and turned its head to focus on Thor.

Brady fumbled at the door lock. "We have to help him!"

Just as he opened the door, Max grabbed him and pulled him back. "No, you – "

Brady punched him in the face. As soon as Max let him go, Brady launched himself out of the SUV to stand right by the door, next to Thor. He raised his arms to make himself look bigger, like you were supposed to do when confronted by a cougar.

Then he did the Tarzan yell.

Confronted with a pair of mammals that had to have been bigger and louder than any it had ever seen, and a ridiculously big car-truck thing, the *Tyrannosaurus* roared again and lumbered off, down the hill, toward Little Buddy Creek.

"Thor!" Brady called as the dog took off after the dinosaur. Thor turned and trotted back.

A moment later, Kyle pressed the button on his key chain and the siren stopped.

As Brady embraced their dog, Nate yelled at him. "You idiot! What were you doing? You could've been killed!"

Kyle looked around. "Everyone okay?"

At that moment, the back door opened, startling them all, but this time, Petra was the only one who screamed.

Nate practically got whiplash looking toward the door just beyond her, though.

It was his dad.

"Boys," he said, "thank God you're home." For the first time Nate could remember, there were tears in his dad's eyes.

Petra punched Nate in the shoulder and then shoved him out of the car and into his father's arms. They embraced and Nate didn't fall onto his face again.

Brady came around the SUV with Thor and put his arm around Nate to help him stand.

Then their dad spoke into the car. "Y'all'd best be off. You have a *Tyrannosaurus rex* to catch."

Max nodded, then leaned out past his grandfather and spoke to Brady, his voice low but intense. "Brady, don't ever go to Ismay High School."

"Bye, Grandpa," Kyle shouted from the driver's seat at the

same time, and roared off down the hill almost before Nate's father closed the door.

As the SUV headed down the hill, following the *Tyrannosaurus* Nate's dad carried Nate into the garage and laid him in the back seat of the station wagon.

"We're taking you to the hospital," he said.

MAX

THE HUMMER SPED DOWN THE HILL AFTER THE T. REX.

"What's going on?" I demanded. I didn't think the others had heard what I'd said to Brady, and I wanted to keep it that way. If they had heard, asking questions about a rogue T. rex would undoubtedly distract them.

"We have to take him home," Emma said, as if it was the most obvious thing in the world. "You don't want a T. rex rampaging through the Lost Pines, do you?"

"But how did it get here? What are those?" I pointed at the kludged-together contraption on the dashboard.

"Uncle Nate solved the mass problem," Kyle said. "It was one of the things he's been doing in London. But it required four Recall Devices."

"We had one of 'em," Emma said, "but we needed three more."

"One of them we got from Grandpa Pierson," Kyle said as we caught up to the theropod. "But two of them were in the Cretaceous. Which was where you came in."

"Wait—how?" I asked.

"One of them was the one you pulled from the water," Emma said.

I leaned forward, having trouble absorbing all of this new information. "But why did you need to do this at all? Why didn't that Recall Device work when I triggered it?"

"The water affected it," Kyle answered. "And it did work. It came back on its own. Uncle Nate rigged it with these so that we could bring the Hummer and pick you all up."

"*You* planned all this?" Petra put in.

"Well, it was mostly Uncle Nate," Kyle said, without taking his eyes off our target.

"But that leaves one more," I said. "Where did that one come from?"

Kyle snorted while Emma suddenly looked sheepish. She swatted Kyle's shoulder and then explained. "That was actually yours. From Mad Jack's cottage."

"What?" I exclaimed.

"Why?" Petra demanded at the same time. "If you'd left it, Max and I could've just come home with Nate and Brady there on the island. And you wouldn't have needed all this!"

"Let's just say," Emma answered, "hypothetically speaking, for the sake of the space-time continuum, that someone might have, or have had, another need of that Recall Device."

"What does that even mean?" I asked.

"That means, baby brother," Kyle said, "that we are not

going to tell you anything more about things you might not have done yet."

"Besides," Emma said, "if I hadn't taken the Recall Device, you might've been out there when the oil tank and generator exploded."

"Wait," Petra said, gripping the back of the seat. "Why *did* the hut explode?"

"An accident," Emma answered, as Kyle shook his head. "No, really. Knob-and-tube wiring from that era. Big fire hazard. It's why they don't use it anymore."

Petra and I exchanged a glance. She shrugged. "She's *your* sister."

"We're going to have to be quick, now," Kyle interjected. "Or else Grandpa Pierson's going to be missing a few cows."

Straight ahead of us was the fence line where the cattle herd was kept. Or at least, it had been kept there in our time.

Then the *T. rex* plowed through the fence, Kyle following, chunks of wood bouncing off the hood and windshield.

"Okay — now!" Kyle shouted, and punched the accelerator. The Hummer surged forward to catch up to the side of the *T. rex*. Ahead, I saw cattle scattering, and then Emma pushed a button on the Recall Devices.

NATE

"DAD," BRADY ASKED AS THEY DROVE UP THE ROAD LEADING OFF the ranch, "what's going on?"

The boys' father looked at them through the rearview mirror. Then he pulled a much-folded, yellowed envelope out of his jacket pocket. "A woman gave this to me at your grandfather's funeral. The two of you would've been around five or six at the time."

Brady snatched it from him and began reading:

Dear Mr. Pierson:

A while back, in the Cretaceous, I met your sons and one of your grandsons under circumstances of which I am not proud. Our families' histories had intersected unfortunately. Nevertheless, they were gentlemen.

Although I left before I discovered exactly what hap-pened to them there, I believe they may have need of a Recall Device, some years before they reach majority.

Signed,

Mrs. Mildred Borski, née Campbell

"Holy . . ." Nate's voice trailed off, and he leaned back on the car bench, staring at the back of his father's head. "So all this time . . ."

"I had a deadline," their dad said. He shifted in the seat. "And I knew I had to make it happen . . . I thought I could do it before y'all got older, but when it didn't happen . . . I should've been there more for you boys . . ."

Nate tried to sort out the details. "So the quadruple Recall Device thing in that SUV. One was from me in the future. One was the one we found in the garage. And one of them was the one you've been working on all this time?"

"Yes," their father replied. "And the other one came from Max himself. But the one from you in the future is actually the same one I'd been working on."

"So all this time," Brady said, "that you've been a great big pile of — "

"Brady!" their dad said.

"I was talking to Nate!" Brady said.

By that point, Nate felt dizzy but strangely happy. He was kind-of-not-really mad at Brady for jumping in front of the *Tyrannosaurus rex*, kind-of-not-really mad at Max for telling them a little but not everything about Brady, and kind-of-not-really mad at his father for, well, everything. But they were family. And his leg was throbbing. "Just get me to the hospital. And don't let them cut off my leg."

MAX

WE EMERGED IN A FAMILIAR REDWOOD FOREST, AND MY BROTHER let out a yell like Han Solo's when they blew up the first Death Star.

We were still beside the *T. rex*, but as soon as we landed, it halted and looked about, confused. Kyle slammed on the brakes an instant later and swung the wheel, spinning the Hummer into a turn and bringing it to a halt, a little too close to the theropod for my comfort.

As I was about to say this, Kyle held up a hand. "Hold on. It's not going to be up for anything else."

Sure enough, the *T. rex* sniffed the air, glanced at the SUV, and then strode off into the forest.

"Let's get out of here," I said.

"We will," Kyle answered, and spun the Hummer around. But instead of activating the Recall Devices, Emma sat back in her seat and we drove on. "Grandpa's going to be okay, by the way," Kyle said. He turned around, flashing a grin. "We checked."

"Oh, good," Petra replied.

I was glad too. Although we hadn't really spent much time with him before his heart attack, I wanted to get to know him better.

"Where are we going?" Petra asked.

Neither of them answered, and we drove in the shadows of the trees and mowed down leafy underbrush. It wasn't long, though, before we reached the river and the sun shone through.

"This looks familiar," I observed.

"It should," Kyle answered, and kept driving. After about ten minutes, he pulled us over.

Uncle Nate — from our time — stepped out from behind a tree.

I opened the door and slid out of the back seat. "What's going on?"

"The VW's pretty totaled," he said, "but I thought I should grab these." He held out his hand. In it were four spark plugs. "The beauty of industrial ceramics. I don't want to risk anyone finding them in our time. The fewer people who know about time travel, the better."

"They won't decay?" I asked. "Because they're ceramic?"

"Probably they will, but I wanted to be on the safe side," he answered. "We do need to collect the bass boat, though."

"Why?" I asked. Sure, the engine had spark plugs, but the rest would rust or decompose in time. Even the fiberglass of the hull.

"Because my dad is going to want his bass boat back," Uncle Nate replied.

< 177 >

I nodded, not really sure what to say.

"Walk with me a moment, Max," Uncle Nate said. We left the others behind and walked along the tree line.

I knew what this was going to be about. "Brady —"

"Went anyway," Uncle Nate said. "Ismay High School and that stadium were built right after he moved out that way. He dated the school librarian there for a while, even went on campus a couple times."

"But —"

"You have no idea the fight we got into when I found out about that." Uncle Nate rubbed an eye behind his glasses. "But Brady lived his life on his own terms." He handed me an envelope, its flap folded in, not sealed. "He wanted me to give you this."

I pulled out the letter.

Dear Max —

It was great meeting you and talking dinosaurs. I wish I were there to see you as you get older. But Nate will be around, and he's good people. If he ever gets out of line, punch him in the shoulder for me.

Uncle Brady

I swallowed and blinked a couple of times before I trusted myself to look at my other uncle.

"For a while," he said, "I blamed you and then him and then

my father and then Mad Jack Pierson and just about everyone else I could think of. But Brady made his decisions. Nothing is pre-ordained."

I thought for a moment. "You said nothing's preordained. Did you ever use your Recall Device to try to — "

"Save him? Stop the fire?" Uncle Nate interrupted. He picked up a rock and threw it out into the river. "Three times, actually."

"And nothing changed?"

"Not in the big picture, no," he answered. Then he half smiled.

"But — "

"Someday," he said, "I'll show you the math."

Author's Note

The Modern Era

The Pierson Ranch is fictional, although its location is based on the Lost Pines area and McKinney Roughs Nature Park near Bastrop, Texas. The geography of Bastrop has been fictionalized somewhat: City Park isn't real but is based on present-day Bob Bryant Park and Fishermen's Park. Also, in real life, there is no boathouse and there are no viewing stands.

Ismay High School and its football stadium are fictional, although epically large high school football stadiums do exist in Texas.

The Mesozoic Era

Borrowed Time is set in Late Cretaceous Texas, in the same era featured in *Chronal Engine*, about sixty-five to seventy-five million years ago. Although certain geographic and biostratigraphic liberties have been taken, most of the flora and fauna are based on the Late Cretaceous Javelina and Aguja Formations of Texas and the Ojo Alamo Formation of New Mexico.

During the Late Cretaceous, sea levels were higher than today, and much of North America (and Texas) was covered by a shallow inland sea called the Western Interior Seaway.

In writing *Borrowed Time*, I've tried to stick to the known fossil record. As of this writing, dinosaurs that are known from fossils found in Late Cretaceous outcroppings in Texas include large tyrannosaurs, such as *Tyrannosaurus rex* and *Albertosaurus;* the sauropod *Alamosaurus;* the pachycephalosaur *Texacephale;* the ceratopsian *Triceratops* (or *Torosaurus*); the hadrosaurs *Kritosaurus* and *Angulomastacator;* the deinonychosaurs *Richardoestesia* and *Saurornitholestes;* the oviraptorosaur *Leptorhynchos;* and nonspecific (smaller) tyrannosaurs, ornithomimosaurs, dromaeosaurs, small ornithischians, nodosaurs, and ankylosaurs. The pterosaur *Quetzalcoatlus* and the crocodilian *Deinosuchus* are likewise known from the Big Bend area of Texas. Although alvarezsaurs are not specifically known from Late Cretaceous Texas, they are known from the same era(s), farther north.

Triceratops and *Ankylosaurus* have not been found in Texas, but the closely related *Torosaurus* and *Euoplocephalus* have, so I've chosen to have Max and Brady describe them by the more common names.

As of this writing, the jury is still out on whether *Nanotyrannus* is a valid genus or whether it is merely a juvenile *Tyrannosaurus rex*. However, there have been reports of a new type of smaller tyrannosaur in Cretaceous Texas (as yet unnamed), so it seems likely that Max would use the *Nanotyrannus* name to describe them.

Mosasaurs are known from the Western Interior Seaway of Texas, although not from freshwater environments. Recently, however, freshwater mosasaurs were discovered from the Cretaceous strata of Hungary, so it is possible there were some in Texas at that time.

Mammals of the era were generally small and included multituberculates, as well as marsupials, such as the possum-like *Alphadon*. Birds would have included some resembling modern forms, but also archaic types that still had teeth.

Beyond that, much of the fauna would have been familiar to a time traveler from today: Reptiles, including lizards, snakes, and turtles, were present, as were amphibians such as frogs and salamanders. Insects and arachnids, worms, and mollusks were present in large quantities.

Sharks and rays would have been present in both freshwater and saltwater environments. Other fish of the era would have included gar, paddlefish, sawfish, coelacanths, and *Enchodus*.

The flora of the era would likewise have been familiar. Large conifers, such as redwoods and cypresses, were present, as were ferns, cycads, and ginkgoes. Trees resembling modern magnolias, palmettos, and possibly oaks were also present. Grasses likely were not, although horsetails were present in marshy areas.

Author's Note

For reading on the science of dinosaurs, an excellent, thorough, and accessible reference is Dr. Thomas R. Holtz Jr.'s *Dinosaurs: The Most Complete, Up-to-Date Encyclopedia for Dinosaur Lovers of All Ages,* Random House (2007). A-to-Z dinosaur encyclopedias are also available from Dorling-Kindersley, National Geographic, Lorenz Books, and Firefly Press.

Finally, Robert T. Bakker's *The Dinosaur Heresies: New Theories Unlocking the Mystery of the Dinosaurs and Their Extinction* (1986) popularized the idea of dinosaurs as active, possibly warm-blooded animals. Much of its analysis remains relevant today, and it offers insights into the state of paleontology in Nate and Brady's era.

ACKNOWLEDGMENTS

Many thanks to the editorial, production, and marketing staffs at Clarion Books/Houghton Mifflin Harcourt. Working with y'all first on *Chronal Engine* and now on *Borrowed Time* has been a pleasure.

Special thanks are due my editor, Jennifer Greene, who regarded a somewhat unprepossessing first draft with a gimlet eye; and to Leigh Wells and Owen Richardson, for awesome interior and cover illustration(s), respectively.

Many thanks as well to my agent, Ginger Knowlton, and the folks at Curtis Brown, Ltd. Thanks also to the Austin and central Texas children's literature community, for support and encouragement on this and other projects.

And, finally, deepest appreciation to my wife, Cynthia Leitich Smith, who not only is my first and best reader, but was also game to (1) watch many really terrible dinosaur documentaries (and some good ones) on cable; and (2) visit, without complaint, every natural history museum in every city we've visited in the past few years.